MAIL ORDER M'LADY

CARRA COPELIN

BookSide Press
877-741-8091
www.booksidepress.com
orders@booksidepress.com

Contents

FOREWORD

Special thanks to Kirsten Osbourne for inviting me to write in her Brides of Beckham world. It has been an honor.

The town of Beaumont, Texas, was a dangerous place to be in 1901. Managers of flimsy boarding houses along the dirt ruts of "Main Street" charged exhausted riggers almost half a day's pay to rent a cot for twelve hours. Enterprising restaurateurs-built fires under 6- foot vats, filled them with water and dried beans, and charged oil hands 15 cents for a cup of "soup." Gas blindness or even gas-induced death was a daily gamble for workers on the seeping rigs. There was also no shortage of gambling and fisticuffs in the ratty saloons. Things got so bad in one Texas boom town that Governor Moody sent the Texas Rangers to settle things down. Safe drinking water was nowhere, and dysentery was everywhere. In short, a boomtown wasn't a healthy place to call home for very long.

Several large fires occurred at Spindletop and in Beaumont during the years following the first gusher in 1901. Reports of a fire on March 4, 1901 recorded that a derrick, a boarding house, and a box car were all consumed by flames that soared several hundred feet high. In 1902, the City installed a large steam whistle atop Eastern Texas Electric Company for fire notification. The number of blasts from the whistle would indicate the box number and location of a fire.

I have used these stories in Mail Order M'Lady to tell what life was like.

INTRODUCTION

Lady Anne Medvale, the daughter of the Marquess of Thamesford, has created a scandal by running away with a prominent politician. In America, alone and penniless, she answers an ad in The Grooms' Gazette and travels to Beau-mont, Texas as a mail order bride.

Morgan Grant, a dedicated cattleman/lawman isn't looking for a wife, but circumstances present themselves and he marries an unlikely mail order bride.

Can the two of them overcome their differences to live happily ever after?

CHAPTER 1

BOSTON, MASSACHUSETTS, OCTOBER 1900

*L*ady Anne Medvale left the office of the bank president. She walked over to her lady's maid who had accompanied her on the cross-town trip.

Without preamble, she said, "Come along, Iris."

Iris O'Donnell joined her, waiting until they were outside on the walk before asking, "What did he say, my lady?"

When she was satisfied no one was near enough to over-hear, Anne answered, "He confirmed the communiqué I received from their establishment last week. There will be no more credit at the bank. We are on our own."

"You had speculated, at the time of your decision not to marry Mr. Ballard, this might be your father's response."

"Yes, but I'm stunned, none-the-less," Anne agreed, "I had hoped he would see reason, and not compel me to marry a man I don't love or force me into a desperate situation. I suppose I should have known better."

Having been born a girl instead of a boy, she'd understood she couldn't inherit her father's title or the estate. She would never have any money of her own, as any monies she inherited would go to her husband. Her father, Henry Medvale, Marquess of Thamesford, had always been more than generous with his daughters, with the assumption that they would someday marry. Margaret and Elinor, both younger, had married last year, fulfilling the family's expectations.

Anne, at twenty-three, was becoming an embarrassment and a liability. There was no one waiting in the wings for her, for evidently, she had spurned one too many suitors. Plus, there was her dalliance with Mr. Smith, which had endangered her reputation and further fueled her father's course of action. Perception was a wicked thing. So, when Harvey Ballard had come for dinner, her father had brokered a deal between the Medvale's and the millionaire American railroad tycoon.

Her father had been so eager to seal the deal that, when the Ballard's had requested the marriage take place in Massachusetts, he had readily agreed. She had opened a line of credit at the bank with her father's letter, when she arrived in Boston this past September. The understanding being, of course, that as soon as she and Harvey Ballard married, she would be his responsibility. Her family would come over for the nuptials in November, and the account would be closed at that time.

Harvey had been nothing but pleasant and attentive on his trips to Higby Castle in the last year. In his own country, however, he was restrictive and intolerant, completely opposite to the man with whom she had become acquainted. She decided quickly she would not subject herself to that kind of treatment, no matter how much money and power he and his family held.

She had said as much to her father, and in his most recent correspondence, he'd insisted she resolve her issues or return to England. She supposed he intended to force her hand, thinking if he dragged her back to England or threatened to cut off her support, she would stop being stubborn and marry Mr. Ballard. His efforts, however, were in vain for that would never happen, nor would she return to Higby Castle.

She'd always heard her father could be a sharp, demanding man in business . . . at times almost cruel. Today, she'd found out first-hand how far he would go to get his way or to make a point.

It was now that her true dilemma began. For the first time in her life, she had to figure out how to survive in a strange country, not only for herself, but also for another person. She was now responsible for Iris, since she didn't have the funds to send her maid back to England.

"I was thinking, my lady," Iris said. "We could stop by the dress shop on our way back to the hotel. You wanted to do some shopping and it might lift your spirits."

"You're right." She smiled and glanced wistfully in the direction of the small dress shop across the street. "A new dress would surely do the trick. Alas, we need to be frugal in our spending, until I decide how we're going to survive. I refuse to go back to England and live under Papa's dominance." She placed her hand on Iris' arm. "I promise you, as soon as I can, I'll send you home."

"My home was Higby castle, and you are my family, my lady," Iris said. "I'm staying with you for as long as you'll let me."

Anne pulled the collar of her less-than-adequate coat around her neck. The clothing they had would have to suffice for now. She hadn't been prepared for the bone- chilling cold weather of this region of the country, and had thought of buying, both she and Iris, heavier wool coats after the wedding. She had managed to put some extra money into her travel safe for emergencies, but the amount saved would barely be enough to cover food and lodging, for who knew how long they had to exist on their own.

What on earth was she going to do? She had no real skills. She had been trained to run a household, plan dinners, and serve on commit-tees. Perhaps she could work somewhere as a seamstress, but only if they needed some fancy embroidery. Their future was bleak indeed.

She glanced at Iris, who stood beside her shivering in her light wool coat. The young woman had become a confidant through the years and she'd come to think of her as more a friend than a maid.

"Iris," she said, interlocking their arms at the elbow. "Our situation is precarious and calls for much deep thought. I dare say we can't do that if we are frozen through. Shall we go back to the hotel to thaw out with a bowl of their hearty stew?"

"That sounds wonderful, my lady," Iris said, with a shudder.

Thankfully, the hotel lobby had a roaring fire in the fire place. They stood near to chase the chill, being careful of their skirts, and then found a table in the dining room.

Once seated and their orders given to the waiter, Anne removed her gloves and continued to consider their plight. She had no plan beyond this meal and their sleep for the night. Their situation was dire, and she had no solution. Then she remembered something.

"Iris?"

"Yes, my lady?"

"Tell me if I'm remembering correctly," she said, "Don't you have family in America?"

"I do, my lady. My relatives are distant cousins living in Texas. But . . ." Iris said, hesitating.

"Yes?"

"They don't know I've traveled to America."

"Iris, I apologize. I've clearly overstepped our boundaries,"

Anne said. "It isn't your responsibility to get us out of the predicament I've caused with my stubbornness."

"A stubbornness that's perfectly understandable, my lady."

Anne wondered about her actions being reasonable. She could fix their situation with a couple of carefully worded letters. Letters that had the potential to ruin her life as she knew it.

Laughter at the next table drew her attention. Two women sat with their heads together, reading what looked like a newspaper. One last giggle between them, and they left the dining room.

Anne noticed the paper still folded on the table. She glanced at Iris and said, "Wish I knew what they were reading that was so amusing. I could use a laugh or two."

Feeling mischievous, she reached stood and grabbed the curiosity off the other table. She returned to her seat and slipped the paper beneath her reticule as their meal arrived. After the waiter left, she spooned a potato from her stew.

"My lady?" Iris raised her hand to her mouth, partially hiding a grin. "What are you up to?"

"My nosiness is getting the better of me, I'm afraid," she said. "I want to read it, but rather than be seen reading something possibly risqué in public, I'll wait until later to read the piece in the privacy of my room."

"It might be embarrassing."

"I doubt it," she said. "But, better to be safe than sorry."

After they'd eaten their meals and retired upstairs to their rooms, Anne tried to take a nap, but the effort was wasted. The paper on the desk across the room called to her like a child demanding attention. She finally gave in and went to the desk. Pulling out the chair, she sat and unfolded the paper, the size of which was no larger than a small magazine.

The title, *The Grooms' Gazette*, topped the page in bold letters. Throughout the booklet were what appeared to be advertisements from men for wives. Some of them were clever or funny sounding and, as she read them, she could see why the ladies might have thought them humorous. But some were also sincere and from the heart. The fact that anyone, either male or female, would need to seek a marital companion in this way was beyond sad and desperate.

Anne thought of her own situation that bordered on desperate, and realized her father, by forcing her hand, had placed her in the same predicament. Suddenly, she understood their motivations and, as she continued to read the entries, she began to form a plan. This surely was the remedy to their dilemma. She started from the first page reading each advertisement until she found the one that intrigued her the most. It read:

To whom it may concern,

Seasoned bachelor needs wife to keep house and husband in smooth running order. I am the City Marshal in the south Texas town of Beaumont. I am of good moral character and prefer lady of same. Would consider pretty a bonus. I am in the fourth decade of life, tall, reasonably good looking, and in good health. Seeking someone willing to be a companion for quiet times.

Homer Rutledge, Marshal, Beaumont, Texas

Her mind churned with the seed of an idea. What if she answered this advertisement? How much worse could it be than her present situation? A knock sounded at the door, and Anne said, "Yes?"

"My lady?"

"Come in, Iris."

The door opened, and after a moment, Iris entered the room carrying a tray with a teapot, cups, and saucers. Anne made room on the side table for the tray and noticed a napkin-covered plate. The fragrance of something freshly baked tempted her nose and her mouth watered.

She lifted the cloth and asked, "What is this?"

"The cook called them sugar cookies. Don't they smell divine?"

"They do, indeed." She put one each on their plates, while Iris poured the tea. Breaking off a piece of the cookie, she popped the bite into her mouth, and said, "These are still warm and delicious."

Iris took a taste and smiled. "Aye, they are."

Anne sipped her tea and glanced toward the gazette lying on the bed. The words of Mr. Homer Rutledge came back to her as if he'd spoken them aloud. *'Seeking someone willing to be a companion for quiet times.'* The more she thought about his proposal, the better sense her idea made.

She poured them both another cup. "Iris, as you said, I too think of you as family. You are closer to me than either of my sisters ever were."

The young woman's cheeks pinked, and she smiled. "We've had some adventures together, 'tis true."

"I'm afraid it goes deeper than that. You know all my secrets." When Iris blushed from the neck up, Anne cleared her throat and continued. "Anyway, I've made a decision concerning our future, and I wanted to tell you straight out, since it involves your future, too." She handed the gazette to Iris, pointed to the advertisement, and waited.

"My lady, this could be worse than the situation with Mr. Ballard. You don't know this gentleman."

"I thought I knew Mr. Ballard, and look how that turned out," Anne said. "I don't see how this could be any worse."

"I'm trying to see your logic, but must we travel all the way to Texas?"

"Yes," Anne said. "Out of all the ones I read, this is the one I like." She went to the desk for paper and pen. Turning to Iris, she said, "Now, what shall we say?"

CHAPTER 2

*A*nne stepped off the train onto the platform of the Beaumont Station. After what seemed an eternity, they'd finally arrived at their destination. Once her feet hit stationary ground, she found herself frozen in place. A bevy of sensations assaulted her, from the hustle-bustle of activity playing out around her, to the pungent, nauseating odor hanging heavily in the air.

As her maid landed behind her, carrying their valises, she wondered again about her decision to accept a marriage proposal from a man she didn't know. Had he had any qualms about placing an advertisement in The Grooms' Gazette? Did he, like her, have no other alternatives?

"Iris, do you see anyone fitting the description of Mr. Rutledge?" she asked. Standing on tiptoe, she scanned the crowd.

"Not yet, my lady," Iris answered, setting the bags at her feet.

"I wonder where he is. The letter said he would be here to meet us."

"We've only just arrived, my lady, and the expedited schedule did put us here a few days early. We don't know if your telegram has even arrived."

"I sincerely hope so. If not, that could be most inconvenient." Anne turned slightly toward Iris with a hesitant smile. "I'm sorry, I'm just a bundle of nerves. You do have the directions stating where we are to go from here?"

"Yes," Iris said. "I have those, and the letter from Mrs. Elizabeth Tandy in my pocket."

"Good, keep them handy until I—"

"Excuse me, little lady, but you're blocking traffic."

A strong pair of hands grabbed her by her upper arms, lifted her off her feet, and then set her off to one side away from the steps. The burly man on the other end of those hands stood a head taller than she and smelled like the stale end of a cheap cigar.

"Well, I never!" Anne exclaimed, struggling for her balance, and a civilized tone. "Take your hands off me!"

At the same time, Iris swung a valise hitting him square in the back, shouting, "Remove your hands from her ladyship at once!"

With obvious surprise, the man let her go, and then threw his arm up to block another assault. Chuckling, he circled Iris's waist with his hands and lifted her, holding her straight out at arm's length. "Ain't you the little spitfire."

"Unhand my maid, you . . . you . . . ruffian!"

Anne's indignant bravado did nothing to improve the man's manners, but she was determined to handle the situation. She had never been treated this way before, nor would she have been if she were still in England. Reminding herself she was in a new country with vastly different behaviors, she changed her plan of attack. Without further delay, she hauled off and shoved him with both fists.

He dropped Iris, unceremoniously, and swung around with a glare. "Who are you to make demands of me?"

Though queasy and trembling, Anne squared her shoulders and faced him. "I am Lady Medvale of Thamesford, and I demand you leave us alone, this instant."

"Well, your ladyship," he said, raising his hand. "I oughta smack—"

"You should do as the lady asks." A stranger calmly spoke up from the edge of the crowd.

"You ain't nobody to tell me nothin'," the ruffian crowed.

The stranger stood steady, and said, "Well, yeah, I am."

"Who says?"

"The city of Beaumont, and these." The stranger pulled his jacket back to reveal a badge pinned to his shirt, and a gun strapped onto his hip.

"Come on, Percy," another man interjected, as he reached out and grabbed the man's arm. "We better get on out to the rig."

The man called Percy chucked Anne under her chin. "We'll be seein' each other again."

"I seriously doubt that," she said, mustering the conviction of every British ancestor she knew.

Percy leered at her from over his shoulder, as he walked away from the station.

Anne gathered Iris over to her side, along with their bags, and glanced at the man who had intervened. He stood several inches taller than she and had shoulders wider than any doorway she'd ever walked through. He wore a black wide-brimmed hat, in addition to the badge, and the gun. She thought he must be what was generally considered a cowboy.

She'd read in western magazines they were rowdy and wild, perhaps not unlike the rude man they'd just encountered, but this one seemed different. Quiet and well-behaved, his calm manner made her think there must be different kinds of cowboys, as there were regular men.

"Ma'am? May I be of assistance?"

"Possibly." She faced him, straightening her clothing. "I'm looking for Mr. Rutledge, the marshal."

"Well, crap," he said under his breath. "We weren't expecting you until next week." He grabbed the handles of the two bags into one hand and supported her elbow with the other. "Here, let's move closer to the depot, and get you ladies off the platform and safely out of the way."

She complied and said, "I'm afraid you have me at a disadvantage, sir. To whom am I speaking?"

"Oh, sorry, I'm Deputy Morgan Grant," he said, setting the bags down, and extending his hand. "It's just that Homer told us where you're from, and with your manner of speaking, I figured you had to be Lady Medvale."

Golly. Perhaps his size had something to do with her perception, but he was the largest and most handsome man she'd ever seen. If Mr. Rutledge was half as handsome, she would be fortunate.

"Deputy Grant." She shook his hand in greeting. "This is my maid, Iris O'Donnell."

He shook Iris's hand.

Anne adjusted the angle of her hat. "Thank you for intervening on our behalf. It's fortunate you were at the station today. Now, if you'll take us to Marshal Rutledge?"

"You're welcome," he said, "I'm afraid it was just luck that brought me here for, as I said, we didn't expect you today."

"Obviously, he didn't receive my telegram explaining our early arrival. I apologize for any undue inconvenience this has caused. If you will get us to Marshal Rutledge, then I won't trouble you any further."

"I'm afraid you aren't going to be staying at the hotel, ma'am. There isn't an empty room for miles. Due to oil being discovered recently at Spindletop, everything's full up."

"I've read about this. I believe it's called an oil boom?"

"Yes, the influx of people hoping to strike it rich has placed quite a strain on the town's resources." He studied the toes of his boots, and said, "Ma'am, you might want to consider going back to where you came from."

"Since Marshal Rutledge knew we were coming, perhaps he's

made prior arrangements for our lodgings."

"It's possible, though I can't speak to what Homer had planned."

"Then I suggest you take me to him, so he can tell me."

His hesitation irritated her, which only added to her mounting frustration. The train's whistle sounded, the conductor shouted, "All aboard!" The wheels of the train began to turn, pulling it away from the station.

Her first instinct was to run and jump on board to leave this God forsaken place, but she couldn't afford one ticket, much less two. She'd spent the last of the money getting her and Iris to this town. She couldn't even afford a room or food for the two of them, as she'd counted on Marshal Rutledge to cover any immediate expenditures prior to their marriage ceremony.

"Deputy Grant is there something you're not telling me?"

"Well, I'm sorry but . . ." The clank and grind of wheel on steel rail covered his words, as the train pulled away from the platform.

A cloud of steam blanketed them, and when it dissipated, she asked, "What did you say?"

Sadness clouded his eyes, and he held her hand in his. "I said, I'm sorry to be the one to tell you, ma'am, but Homer Rutledge is dead."

ANNE HEARD men's voices in the distance, one of them she recognized as belonging to Deputy Grant. He seemed to be defending himself.

"Walt, I told her because I thought she deserved to know."

The other man said, "I'm not disagreeing with you, but bringing her here first might have been better."

"There's no way to soften being told the man you're going to marry is dead."

"I'll give you that one."

A few seconds passed before she heard Deputy Grant speak again.

"Question is, what we do next?"

Slowly, she opened her eyes. She was lying on a narrow bed, inside a small cell surrounded on three sides with iron bars, and a damp cloth cooled her forehead.

Iris appeared by her side, "My lady?"

"W-what happened?" she asked, as she removed the cloth and sat up.

"I'm afraid you fainted at the news about Marshal Rutledge."

Although she could guess, she asked, "And I got here how?"

"Deputy Grant carried you all the way across town."

"Ah, you're awake, m'lady." Deputy Grant stood in the opening to her compartment. "How're you feeling?"

"Embarrassed," she stated, as heat rushed from her neck to her ears. "I've never fainted in my life."

"It's understandable. You had a shock."

"In addition to that," Iris said, "We haven't eaten today."

"That's a problem easily fixed," he said.

"Marshal Fountain has ordered sandwiches from the café."

Anne was certain he heard her stomach growl for, at that precise moment, he looked directly at her and grinned. Was she to be spared no indignation today? She had to get both she and Iris out of here before she was forced to explain their desperate situation.

"We appreciate your kindness, but if you'll just show us to the hotel, we'll get out of your way."

"As I told you earlier, ma'am, the hotels are full up. There isn't a room to be had anywhere in town."

Not that it mattered, she couldn't afford a room if one was available, but that was the last straw. Suddenly, the stays of her corset were too tight. She couldn't draw in enough air, and the room started to spin. She stood, but when her vision blurred, she sat back down on the bed, lest she faint again.

In an instant, he was by her side. He placed his hand on her knee, and asked, "Do you want to lie down?"

"No!" Anne answered hastily.

She glared first at his hand, and then into his eyes. She was unaccustomed to anyone touching her in so personal a manner but saw nothing other than concern. None the less, his touch made her uncomfortable. He must have noticed her discomfort for he removed his hand.

Another thing adding to her uneasiness was the fact she was resting in a place reserved for prisoners. She'd been a prisoner far too long in a rigid system she'd begun to question. A door opened, and she heard voices.

"That must be our lunch," he said. "I'll go get your sandwiches and bring them to you."

"If it's all right, may we join you and your Chief?"

"Yes, if you're up to it." He slipped his hand under her elbow, as she stood, and asked, "How do you feel?"

"Better," she confirmed. "The prospect of food is enough to propel me onward."

"Well then, ladies, I'll lead the way."

She and Iris followed him into a moderately sized room containing two desks, chairs, a bench, and two windows on either side of the door.

A man looked up from the lunch tray and smiled. Quickly, he arranged the chairs for her and Iris to sit where they could use the desk for a table. "Ladies, have a seat."

"Thank you, Marshal . . .?"

"Sorry ma'am," he said, dusting his hand on his pants. "I'm Walter Fountain, City Marshal. Folks call me Walt."

She shook his outstretched hand. "Lady Anne Medvale of Thamesford and my maid, Iris O'Donnell. Thank you for allowing us to rest here."

"I'm glad we had the room. Most days, lately, we're full up. A couple of weeks ago, we had 'em hanging from the rafters. Right, Morgan?"

"Yeah, one night in particular, I thought I was going to have to hammer some nails into the walls."

She took the sandwich offered to her, but try as she might, she didn't understand his reference, so she asked, "Hammer nails?"

"It's something my grandma used to say when all the family came to her house." He grinned, as he sat at the end of the desk, and explained, "When it looked like the beds were going to fill up, she'd say for us not to worry. She'd just hang us by our shirt collars on a nail."

Anne thought that sounded frightful. "Golly, did she . . .?"

"Actually, hang us by our shirt collars? Nah," he said and chuckled. "Occasionally, though, we did line up, eight or ten of us, crosswise on the bed."

"You're teasing me."

"I am, a little." He grinned. "About the nails, anyway. The other is true. In the summer, you didn't want to be in the middle, and in the winter, you didn't want to be on the ends."

"I see." She didn't, of course. She couldn't fathom not having enough room for family or guests. Higby Castle could accommodate many visitors.

They ate in silence for a few minutes, each in their own thoughts. Finally, after she began to feel more like herself, she dabbed her napkin at the corners of her mouth.

"Marshal Fountain? Can you tell me what happened to Mr. Rutledge?"

"I've been debating on how to tell you. It's probably best to say it straight out." He put his plate on the tray and drained his cup of its contents. Looking straight at her, he said, "Homer Rutledge was too trusting. A week ago, he was trying to help settle two men's disagreement and when he got between them, he was caught in the crossfire"

"You mean he was shot?"

"Yes."

"I'm sorry," she said. "He sounded so nice in his letter."

"He was," Deputy Grant said, confirming her opinion. "Homer Rutledge was a good and decent man, and he'll be sorely missed."

"And now, Miss Medvale," Marshal Fountain said. "That brings us to you and Miss O'Donnell. Homer was very private and never discussed his personal business with me or anyone else. I can't imagine you'll want to stay here in Beaumont, so what are your plans?"

Anne glanced at Iris, and then the two men, waiting for her answer. There was no way she could lie or even bluff her way through this. The only way was to tell the truth . . . but only what they needed to know.

She explained briefly about being stranded in America, leaving out her decision not to marry Mr. Ballard of Boston, and the fact she chose to remain in America despite her father's wishes for her to return to England. Reluctantly, she stated her current lack of funds and her inability to afford travel arrangements.

"So, you see, Marshal Fountain, I'm afraid we'll be here indefinitely."

He rubbed his chin like he was in deep thought. "I see your predicament, Miss Medvale, but short of putting you up here at the jail, I don't know how I can help you."

She thought to correct him in the way he addressed her. He should show her the respect of using her title. She supposed, in the grand scheme of things, though, a title meant very little, especially here.

"Please, Marshal, call me Anne." She stood and said, "I appreciate your hospitality today. Iris and I will be out of your way shortly."

"Now, Miss—I mean, Anne, there's no need to rush . . ."

"Thank you, Marshal, I'll figure something out."

Morgan ROSE from his chair as the women left the room for their temporary accommodations of the jail cell. Once they were out of earshot, he sat back down and glanced at Walt whose generous eyebrows were knitted together. Either he was deep in thought or contemplating a trip to the outhouse.

"You know, Morgan," he said after a few seconds, "The answer to both your problems is staring you in the face."

"I'm not following you, Walt."

"Only because you're too stubborn to see the truth right in front of you."

"Who? Her ladyship?" Morgan stared at Walt trying to figure out if he was serious. There was no hint of a smile. "Look, Walt, I don't think—"

"That's right, you're not thinking. Aside from her immediate problems, you need a woman to keep you company out there on your ranch. Besides, you've got that Englishman coming in next month, and she could help you with that."

"Maybe, but I don't know."

"Well, I'm going to make my rounds." Walt stood, reached behind him for his gun belt, and set his hat on his head. He moseyed over to the door, turned, and said, "Seems to me, if you'd give my idea more than three seconds of thought, you'd marry that girl to solve both your problems. Whether she'll have your rusty butt is a different story altogether."

Morgan poured a cup of coffee after Walt closed the door. He recalled all she'd told them about her circumstances. Apparently, she was every bit the lady she appeared to be, from the title all the way down to the soles of her shoes and he'd seen how much her admission had cost her. That title would protect and carry her a long way in England, but it meant nothing here. Without help, there was no way she could survive this town, or any other, on her own.

He had extra rooms at his ranch for both her and her maid, but he wouldn't be returning there until the Texas Rangers arrived to assist Walt in keeping the peace. There was no way he'd leave two women out there alone with his foreman and the one ranch hand he'd left to take care of his place and cattle. Doing so would damage their reputations.

Maybe Walt was right. He *was* tired of talking to himself and that old scruff of a hound that followed him around, besides what could it hurt to have an English wife to make his impending guest feel comfortable and welcome during his stay. The idea seemed solid, so without giving any more thought to the matter, he walked to the makeshift accommodations.

"M'lady?" When she turned and acknowledged him, he said, "I believe I have a solution to your problem."

"Yes?"

"I have a room at the boarding house, and I thought—"

"Surely, Deputy Grant, you aren't suggesting we share your single room at this boarding house?"

"Of course, not, I merely said—"

"Because, I will not allow myself or my maid to be compromised," she said, cutting him off again, her hands clasped together tightly at her waist.

"Trust me, your ladyship," he answered quickly, "The furthest thing from my mind is to compromise you or anyone else.

"I'm the least of your worries where your wellbeing is concerned. There are numerous unsavory characters who would compromise your reputation so fast your head would spin. You encountered one right off the train this morning."

Closing her eyes, she remembered that despicable man, but also avoided his scrutiny while she contemplated her situation and options.

CHAPTER 3

*O*ptions? Who was she kidding? She had escaped disgrace and ruin in her country, only to be faced with a scandal of a similar sort in this one. The only possible option before her was to remain resolute, even though what she wished was to be anywhere in civilization but here. Anne gave his proposition serious thought, and finally said, "All right, Deputy Grant, I'm listening."

He shook his head, gave a half-grin, and then, as if he had another idea, he said, "I can't believe I'm going to suggest this."

She didn't know if she wanted to hear his suggestion or not, but she had no solution of her own, so she asked, "What, pray tell?"

"Iris, may I speak to Anne alone?"

"My lady?"

"It's all right, Iris," she answered. "I'll be fine."

When they were alone, he said, "From listening to your story, it's easy to see you're stuck between a rock and a hard place."

"Go on."

He hung his thumbs in his front pants pockets and continued. "You came here expecting to marry and settle down, and through no fault of your own, you've been stranded with no way to provide for yourself."

She listened to him restate the obvious but said nothing.

"As for me, I've reached a time in my life where I'd like to find a woman to marry, someone with whom to share my life and ranch. I realize I'm not what you bargained for, but I can give you a nice life."

She looked at the gray cloud-covered sky through the window above the bed. While it was true she had made a commitment with another man she had known little to nothing about, saying yes to Morgan Grant would be no different, except they'd had a personal interview instead of a letter. While the fact remained that she didn't have a choice, she didn't respond right away. She didn't want to appear as desperate as she actually was.

"I know you could possibly do better," he said quietly. "But, Anne, what you saw today when you arrived was only a taste of how it would be for a woman alone. At least until the Texas Rangers get here to help restore order.

"If you'll marry me, I promise to keep you safe and well taken care of."

"And, Iris?" She had dragged the poor woman halfway across the world, she wouldn't turn her out now. "Will she be welcome as well?"

"Of course."

She took one more moment before she gave him her answer. "Yes, Deputy Grant, I accept your offer of marriage."

"I think, under the circumstances, Anne, you should call me Morgan."

"All right . . . Morgan," she said.

"Good," he said, "T-t-that's good."

She heard his hesitation. Was he already having second thoughts? Any sane person would. Under normal conditions, the notion of marrying a stranger was absurd. Even with arranged marriages, a couple had a period to get to know each other.

"Well, then, let's get you over to the Mollie B, and introduce you to Mrs. Abernathy," he said. "You can freshen up while I go see if the preacher can marry us this afternoon."

"No."

"No? Why not?"

"No!" She straightened the collar of her jacket and lifted her chin. She remained rock-steady, determined. "I hadn't planned on being married today, and I refuse to be rushed.

"We will marry tomorrow, and you will give me and Iris your room, until other arrangements can be made for her."

"The schedule of events may be out of your control, but I'll see what the preacher has to say. In the meantime, gather your things, m'lady, and I'll escort you to the boarding house."

Anne thought that battle of wills seemed frightfully easy. She wondered if future encounters would be as calm, or if he'd simply given in this time. He didn't come across as the type to let himself be bullied by anyone, much less a woman. No doubt, they had much to learn about each other.

Morgan bristled. He Hadn't Anticipated His Bride-To-Be To Possess A Yes-Sir-No-Sir Type Of Personality, But He Hadn't Expected A Trail Boss Either. In Truth, He Hadn't Known What To Expect. The Letter He'd Found In Homer's Belongings From The Matchmaker, Mrs. Elizabeth Tandy, Had Said His Bride-To-Be Was The Daughter Of The Marquess Of Thamesford, That She Was A Lady Of Quality, And Due To Unfortunate Circumstances, She Wanted To Begin Life Anew.

He didn't know what that meant exactly, and eventually, they would have to talk it through. He assumed she had certain expectations, but so did he. He'd hoped, when he married, to find a woman to share his likes and dislikes and have equal partnership in their marriage. He'd seen the results of a one-sided relationship in his parents' marriage.

His mother had treated her marriage like a business. She was the boss while her husband served as the employee, and it had finally taken its toll. After his father died, Morgan left his mother's home on his fifteenth birthday to escape the oppressive atmosphere. He'd vowed no one would ever run rough-shod over him again. Similarly, he'd sworn always to have respect for the woman he married.

As far as certain attitudes were concerned, better her ladyship show her true colors now, rather than waiting until after they were married. For even though he'd like to have her connections in England for the cattle market, he would forgo them, so as not to spend the rest of his life in misery.

"Shall we collect Iris and go then?" He tucked one of the bags under his arm, while he held the second one in his hand.

"Yes."

Supporting Anne's elbow, he said, "I'll have the rest of your luggage sent to the boarding house later this afternoon."

"Thank you, Morgan. That's very kind of you."

He led them from the police station to the boarding house, where he stayed when in town. Mollie B's was a two- story house that had been converted when Mollie's husband had been killed several months ago in an accident at one of the oil rigs. Ironically, the oil boom that had taken her husband's life, now provided the very support she needed to survive.

Inside the house, he called out, "Mollie?"

"Morgan is that you?"

He greeted the middle-aged woman, who came from the back of the house. Probably the kitchen, he would guess, as she smelled of fresh baked bread and cinnamon.

"Sorry to interrupt your cooking, Mollie."

"It's no problem at all," she said. Wiping her hands on her apron, she smiled, and peered around him. "And, who is this?"

"Mollie, this is Lady Anne Medvale, and her maid, Iris O'Donnell. Ladies, this is, Mollie Abernathy."

Mollie extended her hand. "Anne, Iris, it's wonderful to have you here. I don't mind saying I can use the feminine company." She cut a glance over to Morgan and grinned. "These ranchers and roughnecks can only contribute so much to a conversation."

"I can well imagine." Anne said.

"Come on into the parlor, and I'll fix us some tea."

Morgan didn't know how she achieved it, but Anne managed a smile that was both courteous, and condescending at the same time.

"It's a bit early for tea. I'd appreciate it, greatly, if you could show us to our room. We've had quite a tiring day."

"Well, I . . ." Mollie stammered.

"I know you're tight on space, Mollie," Morgan said, "But if it's all right with you, the ladies can have my room, until the preacher marries us tomorrow. I'll gather my things and move over to the jail for the night."

"I hate to ask you, but that would certainly be helpful."

"It's my turn to stay at the jail, anyway, and give Walt a rest." He turned to Anne and said, "I'll carry your bags to the room at the top of the stairs. You can have it to yourself in five minutes."

He was back downstairs in record time, and found Anne on the settee in the parlor, looking quite pale. Iris fussed about her like a bee buzzing around a fragile flower.

"Are you ill?" he asked.

"No, simply tired from our travels." She stood and walked to the stairs. "I think I'll lie down before dinner."

"I've cleared out, so you should have plenty of privacy."

"Thank you, Morgan." She gave him that same aloof smile.

"Will we be seeing you for dinner?"

"I generally try to get here in time for supper. I don't want to make it any harder on Mollie than is necessary."

"Well then, until later."

Morgan watched her ascend the stairs, back ram-rod straight and her chin tilted upward. Directly, she disappeared behind the bedroom door with Iris right behind her. What was wrong with her, and did that have something to do with why she needed a fresh start? He hated to head down the path his thoughts were taking him, but was he being deceived in some way? Perhaps it *was* best if he took more time to get to know the future Mrs. Grant before they married.

"Thanks, Mollie, for understanding and letting them stay here."

"You're welcome," Mollie said. "As I said, I'll appreciate the female company, but isn't marriage a little sudden? Other that her being English, what do you know about her?"

"Not as much as I'd like. She came here to marry Homer."

"Oh, she's his mail order bride."

"Yes," he said. "Gave her a shock when I told her he'd died. Apparently, she spent all of her money to get here."

"Oh, the poor thing," Mollie commiserated. "But isn't marrying her yourself a bit much?"

"You've been after me for the better part of a year to get married, why're you balking now?"

"Because I meant one of the girls in town, not a stranger."

"Mollie, you know yourself the number of available ladies in the Beaumont area have dwindled quickly, since more men are coming in to drill for oil. The one I had considered early on decided ranch life too isolating and ultimately refused my proposal.

"Homer Rutledge had decided the same thing which is why he placed an ad in the Grooms' Gazette back east."

"I know, but a stranger, Morgan. You don't know anything about her."

"I know she needs help," he said. "And that'll do for now."

"You're a good man, and she's lucky to find you."

"Thanks, Mollie, you're a peach." He reached for her and gave her a hug. "I know she's in good hands."

"Fine," Mollie said and gave him a gentle shove. "Out with you, now. I've got supper to fix."

An hour later, after he'd made his rounds, Morgan entered the law enforcement office. Walt Fountain, sat at his desk amidst stacks of papers, files, and folders. A cigarette dangled precariously from between his lips, while he talked on the telephone, and jotted notes onto a tablet.

Walt hung the receiver onto the hook. "I forgot to ask if you got that incident taken care of at the depot?"

"Yeah," Morgan answered, as he poured himself a cup of coffee. "Turned out to be just a little dust-up. They'd settled it by the time I got there."

He took a drink of something that could only be described as sludge and could have come directly from Spindletop. He wrinkled his face and spit the vile concoction into the spittoon sitting by the desk. "How long's this been sitting on the stove?"

"A while." Walt looked over the rim of his glasses. "Why, does it taste bad?"

"Not if you're going to sell it to Humble Oil." Morgan poured the remainder back into the pot and turned the cup upside down on the shelf. Sitting in one of the two ladder back chairs in front of the desk, he rested his elbows on his thighs, hands clasped together, and asked, "Walt, what time are those Rangers due in here tomorrow?"

Walt pulled a bottle of whiskey from his desk drawer and poured them both a drink. "Got a telegram a while ago saying they've been delayed. They were diverted to Port Arthur, and it may be another week before they get here."

"I see." Morgan drained the glass of the brown liquid, slapped his hands against his thighs, stood, and walked to the door to leave. With his hand on the latch, he said, "Guess I'll get back out there."

"Wait," Walt said, looking up from his paperwork. "Did you talk to Anne?"

"I did. She agreed to marry me."

"Well, that's fine. After you're married, you can take your bride on out to the ranch."

"About that." Morgan turned, his hands bracketing his waist above his gun belt. "I don't have anything definite as far as the ceremony, and I won't leave two women alone at the ranch. I did take them over to Mollie's before I made my way back here."

"Glad you got them settled in."

"I did. Mollie's full up, though, so I gave them my room until we can be married. I thought I'd stay here tonight and give you some time away from the jailhouse."

"That sounds like a deal to me," Walt said. "I'll meet you back here at eight in the morning?"

"That'll do." Morgan gave him a salute and closed the door behind him.

Back out on the street, he wormed his way through the teeming crowd of people, mostly men, from all walks of life. Seemingly overnight, with the discovery of oil at Spindletop, the quiet little town of Beaumont had transformed into a city bursting at the seams with humanity. The crime rate had risen right along with the population, which was the reason Homer had requested help from the Texas Rangers before he died.

Morgan had originally thought about taking his bride-to- be to dinner at the Hotel but being in this horde convinced him they should stay at Mollie's. Besides the inability to navigate the streets due to the number of people, the air was thick with the smell of gas due to the number of wells being drilled. It was unhealthy to breathe when you could smell it, and dangerous when you couldn't. A fire could ignite anytime, anywhere.

Yes, the more he thought about it, the more he believed a quieter, more relaxed atmosphere at Mollie's boarding house would allow them both the opportunity to become better acquainted.

Anne woke to the sounds of banging and clanging, and the rumble of some sort of engine. She got up and walked to the window of her second story room to look out. The view was much better than the one she'd had at the train station. From here, she saw countless numbers of oil derricks protruding from the ground like black metal Christmas trees. The ones closest to the boarding house had men climbing back and forth, and up and down, like ants on their leafless branches.

A whistle, in the distance, announced the arrival of another train, just as a light knock sounded on her door.

"Yes?"

"It's Iris, my lady."

"Come in." Anne turned and smiled as her maid came into the room. Sitting at the dressing table, she asked, "How long did I sleep?"

"Just about an hour, my lady," Iris said, while smoothing the covers on the bed.

"Was Mrs. Abernathy able to find you a place to stay, while we're here?"

"Yes, she has a small room off the kitchen that's quite suitable."

"You know I'm perfectly willing for you to stay here with me. We've certainly had our moments together over the past few months." She had offered to share the room with Iris, even though she knew the young woman would never breach that line of demarcation between their social status.

"I know, my lady, but I've already placed my things in there." Iris finished making the bed, and freshened Anne's hair style. "Would my lady like to change out of your traveling clothes?"

"No, I think I'll wait and change for dinner. It will make for less trouble for both of us."

"Very good, my lady." Iris placed a pearl encrusted, butterfly-shaped comb into the curls fashioned atop Anne's head, and stepped back. "Mrs. Abernathy has tea ready in the parlor, if you'd like to join her."

"Why, yes, I believe I would. My stomach might be able to handle it now." She checked her reflection in the mirror and smoothed the wrinkles in her skirt. Straightening her jacket, she set off to join Mrs.

Abernathy for tea.

Downstairs, Anne observed her surroundings with a discerning eye. The boarding house gave her the feeling of a home rather than a place that rented rooms. There were personal photographs strategically placed around the parlor, and a few exquisite items decorated the shelves.

She was accustomed to expensive heirlooms, but most had no real connection to her. The paintings, furniture, and fixtures in the castle where she'd grown up, were from too many generations ago for her to care much about.

"Oh, here you are. Have a seat, and I'll pour you a cup." The woman she'd met earlier sat in one of two chairs separated by a small round table. The tea service rested on the table on a tray.

"Thank you, Mrs. Abernathy, that would be lovely."

"Please, Anne, call me, Mollie."

Anne winced inwardly at the woman's use of her given name. In England, only a family member would have addressed her without using her title. To anyone else, she would've been Lady Medvale, Lady Anne, or your Ladyship. She'd learned, though, since she'd been in America, people were more familiar, and titles weren't used.

She had also learned, since being on her own, that friends were a good thing to have and at a premium. It seemed prudent not to alienate the ones who stepped forward.

She smiled. "How very kind."

Anne sipped her tea, and the warmth spread through to her fingertips, giving her a snug feeling of home. She smiled and said, "You make a wonderful cup of tea, Mollie."

"Thank you, I learned from my grandmother." The woman sipped from her cup, her cheeks turning a pleasant pink at the compliment. "She was from England with an Irish heritage, so if nothing else, I learned how to brew a good pot of tea. Oh, and by the way, I have drinking water in the kitchen. Before you go upstairs for the night, I'll fix you a pitcher to set by your bed.

"When Mr. Abernathy built the house, he had it fitted with indoor plumbing. The toilets are nice, but the water for drinking or cooking is tainted due to the drilling. It's soupy, and its odor clearly smells of fish, bullfrogs, and alligators. If you drink it before it's been boiled, you'll likely develop severe stomach cramps, or what we call, a case of the Beaumonts."

"Heavens, it sounds dreadful. Your warning will be heeded. I'll be sure to tell, Iris."

"We spoke earlier while you were resting. She said she experienced a similar problem while on board the ship."

"That's true, she did. At one point, she could barely manage to help me with my corset."

"A tragedy, indeed, your ladyship."

Anne snapped around at the sound of a male voice. Her future husband stood in the doorway, hat in hand, and more handsome than any man she'd ever seen. His eyes, dark with an almost turquoise hue, stared at her as if she'd suddenly sprouted an extra set of ears. His mouth, while possessing lips that looked soft, spoke words that dripped sarcasm.

Unaccustomed to being provoked, she rarely felt the need to explain herself to anyone, and she wouldn't now, especially to a man she barely knew. She stood and set her cup and saucer onto the tray. "Mollie, thank you again, for the tea and conversation. What time is dinner?"

"Food will be on the table at six o'clock. I'll let you know when it's ready."

"I appreciate it, but I—"

"By all means, let's cater to her ladyship," he interrupted.

"Morgan," Mollie said, as she snapped her fingers, and pointed to the settee. "Sit down."

Anne bristled, narrowed her eyes, and glared at him. "I was going to say, there's no need, I have a timepiece." To Mollie, she said, "Don't worry, I'll be down at six, sharp."

As she ascended the stairs, Anne wondered, once again, about her decision to become a mail order bride. Goodness knew, it wouldn't be the first time she'd made a wrong choice.

MORGAN HAD over-stepped with his confrontational attitude toward the woman he was to marry. He knew it, as well as he knew he was about to be on the receiving end of a tongue lashing from Mollie Abernathy. More like an older sister to him, she had no problem sharing her opinions.

"All right," she said, after closing the doors to the parlor, "What's the matter with you? Where are your manners?"

"I—"

"And don't say you don't know," she cautioned, as she joined him on the settee. "You've never had any trouble saying exactly what you meant. Now what's put that burr under your blanket?"

He huffed out his frustration in a heavy sigh. What was it about Lady Anne Medvale that rubbed him the wrong way? She was as pretty as any woman he'd ever seen. Anyone could see she came from money, with her fine dresses, jewelry, and fancy manners. She hadn't done anything to him, but . . . he just couldn't figure it out.

"Maybe it's her tone" he answered. "Her arrogance and that air of superiority sets my teeth on edge."

"I think she's scared to death," Mollie said, "And why wouldn't she be? All alone in a town that's gone crazy, not to mention a strange country." Mollie placed her hand on Morgan's arm. "Why don't you two have your cake and coffee here, in the parlor, this evening? Take some time to get to know each other before you marry."

"I guess it couldn't hurt."

"I'd say not," Mollie said. "Give her a glimpse of the good man I know you to be."

He stood, picked up his hat, leaned down to kiss her cheek, and then walked to the door. "Can I bring you anything?"

"Just a better attitude."

With a tip to the brim of his hat and a grin, he said, "I'll see if I can dig one up."

AFTER A DINNER OF BAKED CHICKEN, roasted potatoes, and biscuits, Morgan escorted Anne into the parlor. He rather wished they could sit outside on the porch but, in addition to the odor, the night air had a nip to it. As she sat on the settee, he stirred the logs in the fireplace to bump up the heat in the room, and then sat in an upholstered side chair across from her.

"Mollie's supper was good." His words sounded as stiff and dull as he felt and was as poor a conversation starter as he'd ever heard.

"Yes, it was delicious."

"Are you comfortable enough in your room? Do you have everything you need?"

"I've settled in well enough and, thanks to Mollie, Iris has found an adequate spot downstairs."

Her voice took on that snooty tone again, and he clenched his teeth tightly. He'd thought the room large enough for the two women but, evidently not. Since neither woman seemed to have their nose out of joint over the situation, he stopped himself before confronting her. Obviously, there were vast differences in the way they'd been raised. He supposed this was why Mollie had said the two of them needed to talk.

"I'm glad to hear it."

Silence hung heavily between them like the velvet drapes that covered the windows. Not being much of a talker, he supposed he should asked her about England, but she managed to beat him out of the gate.

"Are you originally from Texas, Morgan?"

"Yes, but a bit further north of here, around Austin."

"And have you been here in Beaumont long?"

He cleared his throat, uncomfortable talking about himself, but answered, "I've been here about ten years."

"I read somewhere the ranches in Texas could be quite large. What size is yours?"

"Excuse me?"

"How many acres do you own?"

"Well, I . . ." He hesitated unsure as to how to answer. Perhaps she was accustomed to blurting out the state of her finances, but he wasn't. He came close to telling her she was rude and insulting but, in the sense of getting along, he held onto that thought. "I'd say it's pretty good size. Compared to some of the larger outfits, though, it's on the smaller side."

"I'm sure you feel I'm prying, Morgan, but if I'm to know anything about the man I'm going to marry, I have certain curiosities." She lifted her chin and smiled. "Surely you have questions of your own?"

"I do."

"What would you like to know?"

"Why are you here?"

"I don't know what you mean?"

By the look of confusion on her face, he could tell he'd unsettled her. Maybe there was a real woman beneath that prim and proper façade after all.

"I mean, what was so bad at home that you abandoned your family and privilege for a life in a foreign country?"

"I simply thought it time to seek adventure. My life in England had become dull and boring, and I thought, why not?"

"Just like that?"

"Just like that."

And, just like that, the façade was back in place.

CHAPTER 4

Anne knew, eventually, she'd have to tell him the real reason for abandoning her home and country. She absolutely couldn't tell him about the scandal hanging over her head, yet, at least not before they wed. What would she do if he refused to marry her? She had no other place to go and, even if she did, she had no money to get there.

She also knew, if she were to maintain an equal footing in this marriage, she needed to keep him slightly off-balance. She remembered her grandmother saying, *never let your husband think he has the upper hand.* His constant stare unsettled her, as she assumed he meant to do, so she studied the floral pattern of the parlor rug, while garnering her strategy. Lifting her head, she met him with equal intensity.

"Tell me, Morgan, what are you looking for in a wife?"

"Well, I, umm . . .," he hesitated, as if searching for the words. "I've reached a point where I need someone to help me navigate the social waters. You see, my cattle business has become more prominent, and I'm less refined than I should be."

"Certainly, you're better equipped than you think. Are the

standards here more rigid than I imagined?"

The sound of her own words bounced back to her off the hard planes of his features. His taught jawline and narrowed brow told her she should temper her attitude. She had much to learn, if she intended on making a success of this union.

She attempted to make light of her previous question and smiled. Teasingly, she asked, "Do you have a reputation I should be aware of?"

He had the grace to appear slightly chagrinned. "I've been rowdy in my younger years, got into a little trouble here and there. Mollie's been working to chisel my sharper angles."

"I see. So, other than me further honing your rough edges, what are your expectations from this union?"

"I guess I'm hoping we can be mutually beneficial to each other."

"Of course, but, in addition to our original prospects, what are you hoping for?" She was being bold, but she needed him to state the obvious. When he didn't, she asked, "Will this be a real marriage between us?"

He glanced at his boots, briefly, then met her gaze head on. "That's my hope. Are you up for that, your ladyship?" he taunted. "A real marriage?"

Her body temperature rose exponentially, surpassing that of the room, and yet, she shivered. He'd deliberately goaded her. Whether she took the bait was up to her. She'd never been good at games, especially those played between men and women. Her lack of experience and knowledge in this area was precisely what had gotten her into trouble with Mr. Smith.

"I believe, after a respectable period, we can reach a suitable agreement," she said.

"A respectable – what does that mean? Six months? A year? Ten?"

"We don't know each other, Morgan. We've barely met, much less courted. How do we know if we're compatible . . . in that way?"

He stood and paced in front of the fireplace. Suddenly, he

crossed over to her, lifted her off the settee, and pulled her close. "I can tell you in ten seconds."

Anne met him face-to-face with only token resistance. Her mind screamed at her to put up a struggle, but her body overruled any conscious thought she may have had. When his mouth covered hers in a kiss that took her breath away, she lost even her initial urge to resist. What started out as forceful, softened into a rather sensual experience. One that she didn't want to end.

When he broke their kiss, he still held her close, staring into her eyes with a longing that weakened her knees. Breathless, she whispered, "Golly."

"I suppose I should head on over to the jail," he said. "It's my turn to give Walt the night off."

Something happened with that kiss. He seemed less rigid and his voice had lost most of its bluster. She swayed, slightly off-balance, when he released his hands from her shoulders. Resisting the urge to sit, she said, "Yes, it's getting late."

He walked to the parlor door, opened it, and turned to face her. "Goodnight, m'lady. Sleep well."

As he left through the front door, her fingers touched her lips and she wondered if that was even possible.

MORGAN WAVED GOODBYE TO WALT, as he left the jail, and sat behind the desk. He sifted through the stack of reports in front of him but found he couldn't concentrate. A certain straight-laced, ebony-haired, aristocrat kept invading his thoughts.

Tonight, he'd glimpsed the woman behind the façade. His lips still tingled from their kiss. Yes, a fire definitely smoldered beneath her surface. How long would she hold him at arm's length before allowing him to stoke that fire?

Their shared kiss hadn't lasted that long, but it had been long enough to cause his body to respond. Even now, the anticipation of tasting her again sent his imagination on a wild ride. Before his thoughts overtook him, he leaned to his right, pulled open the bottom drawer, and removed the bottle of whiskey and a glass.

Before too long, he'd need to make a walk around town, but in the meantime . . . He poured two fingers of the caramel colored liquid into the glass and downed the shot in one gulp. Pouring another round, he rested his booted feet, crossed at the ankles, on the corner edge of the oak desk and sipped at the second drink.

He closed his eyes to let the warmth of the whiskey relax his over-active imagination, then suddenly, gunshots rang out in the direction of one of Beaumont's several saloons. His boots hit the floor. He stood, checked his Colt Peacemaker, and hurried out the door onto the wooden sidewalk.

A crowd had already gathered in front of Beasley's Watering Hole, and as he came closer, he realized they had surrounded a body lying wounded in the street. Pushing through the throng of people, he finally reached the familiar form. Walt Fountain lay sprawled in the dirt with a gunshot wound in his left shoulder.

A voice shouted above the crowd noise, "Somebody get Doc Harper!"

Morgan glanced over to Jacob Beasley, who was pressing a bar towel onto Walt's wound to slow the bleeding.

"Jacob, did you see who shot him?"

"No, but I have a pretty good idea." The man shifted his position and explained, "Walt had been trying to cool down one of those hot-headed roughnecks who'd riled up a table of card players."

"Would you recognize him if you saw him again?"

"Yeah, I could probably pick his surly hide out of a crowd."

"Good, I'll—"

"Deputy Grant?" Beasley's son, Junior, slid to a stop at Walt's feet. "Doc said we should bring Marshal Fountain over to the office where he can get a better look at him."

"Jacob, you're in charge of rounding up witnesses and taking statements. I'll be back when I can." Morgan shifted around to Walt's head and slipped his hands under the man's shoulders. "Junior? Grab his legs."

"Yes, sir."

Once they'd lifted the big man, he asked, "Got a good hold of him?"

"Yes, sir, I do."

"Then watch where you're walking and let's go."

Morgan and Junior reached Doc's office and followed him to the back room where he performed his surgeries. After they laid Walt on the table, Morgan sent the boy back to his pa, and waited for Doc's assessment.

Finally, Doc looked up and commented, "You staring at me isn't going to make me work any faster, you know."

"Is he going to be all right?"

"I believe so, but I can't go digging around, willy-nilly if he's going to use this arm in the future." Doc cut the shirt off Walt's body and began cleaning the area. "I've sent for Mollie to help with the surgery, and we'll get word to you when we're done. Now, don't you have some investigating to do?"

"You're right, Doc, thanks."

Morgan left out the back just as Mollie arrived, and he held the door for her. She appeared calm, as she always did, but worry lines etched her face. He knew Walt had taken to visiting her of late, and hated she had to help Doc with the surgery.

"Mollie, I'm sorry you're the one that has to help. I know you've become fond of Walt over the last few months."

"That's true, but it just so happens, I'm the best nurse Doc has ever had." Her cheeks turned rosy. "I'll go take care of Walt, if you'll go find the S.O.B. who did this to him."

"I'm on my way." He dipped his head a fraction, touched the brim of his hat, and headed to the street toward the Watering Hole.

He caught sight of Jacob and a few other men across the room, as he stepped through the swinging doors, and walked straight to them. "What do you have, Jacob?"

"Out of the fifty or so in here at the time of the difference of opinion, only a handful or so were willing to leave a statement and a name." He handed Morgan the few pieces of paper with the statements. "Most are fairly new to town and haven't developed any loyalties to local folks."

"It should only be a matter of right or wrong," Morgan said, as he read a couple of statements, "But, I guess most are leery of getting involved."

"Wish I could've been more help."

"I appreciate what you've done. Just keep your eyes and ears open, and get word to me, as soon as you can, the next time you see him."

"I will."

Morgan stuffed the witness statements into his shirt pocket. He gazed around the room. Of the handful of men who remained, only one or two of the faces were familiar. He hoped, with a little sleep and with the light of day, folks' memories would improve, so he could track down the marshal's shooter.

Anne removed her gloves, handed them to Iris, and then sat on the stool, in front of the mirror. She removed her earrings and necklace, handing each to Iris in turn. Next, she would step out of her shoes, dress, and underthings, and then accept her nightdress and wrapper from Iris. Methodical. From birth, her entire life had been disciplined. No thinking required.

She had never pushed a boundary until she'd followed Mr. Smith to London. Everything changed with that one fateful decision. She had heard rumors about his philandering, but he'd been completely respectful of her position. At the time, she hadn't considered her trip to London a rebellion, but, in retrospect, it was bold for a lady of her stature.

And now, she was here, a full continent away from everything she knew, and everyone she loved. Iris's voice pulled her out of her thoughts.

"My lady?"

"What is it?"

"When you're ready, I have your nightdress."

Anne realized she'd been absorbed in her own feelings without regard for Iris. They'd shared the same day, and she was likely every bit as tired. "I apologize. Yes, of course, you'd like to go to bed."

Iris smiled. "Aye, but not until you're snug beneath the covers. Now here you go."

When she'd slipped on her nightgown, Iris helped her with the wrapper, and proceeded to place her things into the armoire. She watched the young woman, not much younger than herself, put everything carefully away. Anne walked over to the bed where the sheets and blankets had been turned down.

She fingered the crocheted lace edging of the sheet-top, and asked, "Have we made a mistake, Iris?"

Iris set the shoes onto the floor of the armoire, straightened, and joined her. "In what way, my lady?"

"In leaving England, and all we know, to end up in such a dismal place." Anne climbed onto the bed and drew her knees up, encircling them with her arms. "I feel like I've forced you into making a decision that's ruined your life."

"While I agree this is far from what we had in mind, when you answered the gentleman's ad for a wife, we didn't arrive at this decision lightly. We came to the conclusion this was the best way to handle your situation. Eventually, I'll join my relatives in Dallas."

"I wish I was more certain."

"Don't worry, my lady," Iris assured, "It will all work out. Mollie really likes your Mr. Grant."

"I wish I did."

"It won't be easy for either of you. You're both traveling an uncharted path."

"It's true, we have absolutely nothing in common." Anne slid her feet beneath the covers as a knock sounded on the door.

Iris hurried over, and asked through the wood partition, "How can we help?"

"Ma'am? I'm Jacob Beasley's son, and I have a message for Lady Medvale from Mrs. Abernathy. Can I slide it under the door?"

"Aye."

Anne watched as a folded piece of paper materialized from beneath the door. Footfalls sounded on the stair treads, and then the heavy front door to the house slammed shut. She took the note from Iris and began to read the hurriedly written missive aloud.

Anne, the marshal has been shot in the street. I'm going to help Doc Harper with the surgery. I don't know how long I'll be, possibly all night. Morgan will be the marshal until Walt returns or until the Rangers show up. I'll let him know, as soon as I can, that you and Iris are alone in the house with the other borders. Sorry for the trouble, Mollie.

"Crikey," Anne whispered, looking at Iris, "I hope he'll be all right."

"So, do I," Iris responded. "I hope this doesn't place Mr. Grant in more danger."

"I hope that, as well, but I suppose it does." She pulled the covers up and settled against the pillow. "We should both get some rest, as I expect tomorrow will be full of unknowns. Goodnight, Iris."

"Goodnight, my lady."

CHAPTER 5

$\mathcal{M}$organ turned the knob on the back door of Mollie's boardinghouse, replaced the key beneath a milk can, and stepped through the entrance. Evidently, Walt had convinced her to start locking her doors, next they'd have to get her to hide the key in a less obvious place. One step at a time.

The kitchen was dark and quiet. The ticking of the clock in the parlor, on the fireplace mantle, the only noise. When it chimed five times, he sighed, and said under his breath, *"Doggit, no wonder I'm tired."*

Movement to his left caught his attention but, before he could reach for his Colt, something substantial glanced the side of his head. He reeled for a second, but thankfully, with his eyes more accustomed to the dimness, he saw the second assault coming, and grabbed the arm of his attacker. Head pounding, he carefully removed a cast iron skillet from the assailant's hand. One he recognized.

"Anne?"

"Oh . . . it's you!" She fell against him. "I didn't know, I just heard a noise."

Morgan wrapped her into his arms and held her tightly. She shook so violently, he wondered if she would fly into bits and pieces.

"What are you doing down here in the dark?"

"I-I couldn't sleep and came down to fix some tea." She tightened her arms around his waist. "I heard someone at the back door and grabbed the nearest thing to use as a weapon."

"Resourceful," he commented. He touched his temple, winced, and grinned as his fingers came away slightly bloody. "Very efficient."

"I'm so sorry, I never meant to hurt you."

"I'm all right, you did good."

"My lady?"

Morgan looked up to see Iris holding a lamp and gripping a kitchen knife, standing in the doorway to what was usually Mollie's sewing room. "Miss O'Donnell, sorry to have disturbed you."

"Mr. Grant, thank the angels it's you. Are you all right, my lady?"

"Iris, yes, I'm fine." She pushed away from Morgan. "I came downstairs to fix some tea, and I—"

"Smacked me upside my head with a skillet."

She faced him squarely. "I said I was sorry for that, you should've gone to the front door. Why were you coming in so late anyway?"

"I'd been pouring over witness statements, and lost track of time. After I checked on Walt, I thought I should stop here and make sure you were doing all right."

"Oh, I see. Well, then, Iris, would you put the kettle on to boil?"

"Of course, my lady."

"In the meantime, Morgan, sit down." Anne reached for a towel to wet it with water, from the pitcher sitting on the counter. "I'll clean that wound on your head."

He started to protest, but decided he'd rather have a caring, apologetic Anne, than a distant, aloof Lady Medvale. He sat in the nearest chair and tilted his head back at an angle.

Moving the lamp closer, he asked, "How's that?"

"Better." She dabbed the wet cloth at his wound. "Again, I apologize for swinging at you."

"And hitting me – you did hit me."

She bristled. "I would think, by now, a gentleman would accept my apology and let the incident drop."

Her fingers trembled at his temple, and he had a pang of remorse. He knew he should let it go. Why he couldn't, escaped his conscious thought. He was learning what ruffled her and what made her withdraw behind her aristocratic façade. He decided her retreat was her protective mechanism to keep people from getting too close, or maybe to cover her inability to interact.

"This is why I need you." He raised his hand and covered hers quickly before she had a chance to pull away. Her eyes, the color of rich mahogany, met his with a directness he admired. "I need you to mold my rough edges into a gentleman . . . or a reasonable facsimile. Can you do it?"

"I'll most certainly try."

"That's all I have a right to ask." He pulled her closer. Her breath came in short, quick pants, and her heart beat wildly in the hollow at the base of her throat. Finally, he asked, "Where do you suggest we start?"

"I . . . y-you," she stammered, "Should accept my apology."

"That's first, huh?" He leaned even closer, fully expecting her to back away, but she remained rock-steady.

"Yes."

"Well, then, your ladyship," he said, with a grin. "I accept your apology."

"Tea is ready, my lady." Iris set the pot in the middle of the table, along with cups and the fixings. "Mr. Grant, may I get you anything else?"

Morgan cleared his throat, let go of Anne's hand and answered, "No, thank you, Iris. Sit with us and have some."

"No, thank you, sir. I'll go back to my room." She curtsied, and then turned to go.

After a slight hesitation, Anne said, "Please, Iris, join us for some hot tea. Goodness knows, you probably need it, after being woken up out of a sound sleep.

"If you're sure, my lady, I would enjoy a cup."

"Good, I'll pour." Anne set the pot back on the table, stirred in some sugar to her own drink, and asked, "How is Marshal Fountain?"

"He's resting. Doc Harper thinks he'll recover full use of his left arm."

"That's good news." She sipped from her cup. "And, Mollie? I'm sure she's tired out."

"Yes, but I doubt you'd ever hear her say it out loud."

"I've only known her for a day, but I agree with you. Iris and I will go see her later this morning at the doctor's office."

Morgan pushed his chair away from the table and stood. "I guess I'd better get back to the jail. I need to check on the few prisoners we locked up last night."

"Can't anyone else do that?"

"No, it was me or Walt tonight, and with him laid up over at Doc's, I have to get them food and a walk to the outhouse."

Morgan rested his hand on the front door knob. He had one more thing he needed to talk with Anne about, but had no idea how she'd take what he had to say. She could either be relieved at the turn of events, or mad as a wet barn cat.

"Anne," he said, facing her, and taking hold of her hand. "I don't know how you'll feel about it, but I've found out the preacher is out of town for a few days. We'll have to wait to marry until he returns. Beyond that, we'll continue as we've been doing, with you here at Mollie's and me at the jail until the Texas Rangers get here to help enforce the law."

"Oh . . ." she answered softly. "How long will that be?"

"I don't know exactly when they'll get here, but I'll need to stay on the job until they do. Until Walt recovers, me and the other two deputies will be busy watching over the town."

He shifted his stance and glanced at her doe eyes staring back at him intently. Talking to her would be so much easier if he could get a read on her. He'd never known anyone who kept their feelings so deeply hidden. She was wrapped as tight as a new rope.

He cleared his throat, and continued, "Obviously, I'll set up accounts for you at the mercantile, the dress shop Mollie uses, and the café on Main. If there's anything else, don't hesitate to ask me. I want you to have everything you need."

"Thank you, Morgan, that's very kind."

"Well, it's the least I can do. Say, when I go to the stores this afternoon, would you like to accompany me and meet some folks?"

"That would be lovely."

The fingers on the hand he held trembled and were cold as ice. "Anne, are you all right?"

"Yes, why wouldn't I be?"

"I don't know, it's just . . . you seem . . ." He still didn't know her well enough to speculate. *I don't know her at all.* After a second or two, he finished, "Never mind. I'll see you around lunchtime."

He took one last glance, squeezed her hand, put on his hat, tipped the brim, and headed toward the marshal's office. This getting to know someone was much more difficult than he ever could've imagined.

ANNE LISTENED as his boots left the porch, hit the rock path, and continued until out of earshot. Movement upstairs told her the other boarders were awake and beginning to stir. She rejoined Iris in the kitchen, who, by then, had cleared the table of the cups, saucers, and teapot.

"Iris, do you know how to cook?"

"I can put a few things together for a meal, my lady, what do you have in mind?"

"I was wondering how best to help Mollie," she said, tapping her cheek, "And, I believe I know how."

"What's up your sleeve, my lady?"

Anne went to the pantry, pulled out two loaves of bread, and two jars of jam. In the ice box, she found milk, bacon, and butter. Next to that, on the drainboard, sat the basket of fresh eggs.

"The other boarders will be down soon expecting breakfast. Do you think we can take care of them for her?"

"I've never been a kitchen maid, but I can fry bacon, and my mother used to make us pan toast."

Happy to be useful, Anne took charge, and said, "Good, I'll set the table, and ready the buffet for the food, and then I'll come in to scramble eggs like Cook taught me."

Iris giggled. "Did her ladyship know you were skulking around downstairs?"

"No, and I doubt she ever will, now." Warm tears welled in her eyes and threatened to fall. "That ship has sailed – literally. I can't imagine ever seeing Ma-Ma again."

"One day, my lady, this will all be forgotten, and you'll be back home."

"Not if Pa-Pa has any say in the matter, I won't." She grabbed an apron from the hook by the back door, but as she started to tie it at her waist, realized she was still in her nightgown and wrapper. Laying it across the chair-back, she looked at Iris. "Crikey, we'd better go dress, or the Mollie B will go from a boardinghouse to a house of ill repute before breakfast."

"You're right about that." Iris concealed a giggle with her hand. "We could really start the tongues to wagging. I'll be right up to help you."

"There's no need, I'll manage this morning. Go ahead and get yourself ready."

Iris nodded. "My lady."

All the way up the stairs, Anne thought about her predicament of being here alone, and penniless. But all that paled with the shooting of Marshal Fountain. He and Mollie were her first friends in this strange town of Beaumont, and she would do anything for them. Even trying to cook. She would survive in spite of her father's coldness.

In her room, she gathered her clothes for the day. Their trunks hadn't arrived as expected, but even if they had, she realized how inappropriate they were for what she needed on a day-to-day basis, much less this morning. It was fair to say she had nothing remotely suitable for life on a ranch either.

She had noticed Mollie dressed in a style of fashion that was more relaxed, without the requirement of a corset. She would speak to her when she came home and ask for guidance. Thank goodness her intended groom had offered to open a few charge accounts for her. His gesture would save her a great deal of embarrassment and afford her the means to purchase a proper wardrobe.

She looked forward to their outing this afternoon, and the opportunity to learn more about the man she was to marry. He'd made references to his rough edges, but she hadn't seen anything so terrible. Morgan Grant was no English gentleman and never would be, but no one was perfect. There was always room for improvement.

Back to the task at hand, Anne chose her garment for the day and managed to get everything laced and buttoned on her own. She made her way downstairs just as Iris set a plate of sliced bread on the table. No one gave her a second look but continued passing around a platter of fried eggs and bacon.

She found Mollie at the stove frying more eggs. "Mollie, you're back. How is the marshal?"

"He's not out of the woods yet," Mollie said, wiping her brow. "The doc removed the bullet though and, if his fever goes down, he should recover."

"That's good news. What can I do to help?"

"If you'll take the pot around and refill their cups, I'll take these last eggs in, and we'll be done for a bit."

Mollie grabbed her arm as Anne reached for the large pot on the stove. "Wait!" she said, quickly handing her a folded towel. "Use this or you'll burn your hand on that hot handle."

"Thank you, Mollie. That was careless of me."

"Not to worry, I'll watch out for you."

Anne picked up the coffee pot and carried it into the dining room with Mollie right behind her. The few that were left, finished their meals, and said their goodbyes. She helped Iris stack plates and took them to the kitchen.

Mollie sat at the small kitchen table and said, "Come on, girls, join me for a spell. You put in some hard work and deserve a rest."

"You're the one who should lie down after being up all night." Anne poured Mollie a cup of coffee and joined her. "I hope you are right about the marshal recovering. I pray he does regain the use of his arm."

"If Walt does what Doc Harper says, he should make a full recovery. I've offered to have him stay here so I can tend to his wound easier, hopefully he won't raise too much of a ruckus." Mollie yawned and smiled. Standing, she glanced around the room. "I believe I will lie down for a while. Don't worry about this mess, I'll clean up when I come down to fix dinner."

As soon as Mollie left the kitchen, Iris began to put food away. Anne cleared the table of the dirty dishes, removed the tablecloth and napkins, and put a kettle of water on to boil.

"My lady," Iris said, "go put your feet up. I'll take care of this."

"No, I'll help." When Iris started to protest, Anne said, "It's all right. We're in a different situation here, and I will have to adapt and adjust. I may not be able to cook, but I can certainly wash a dish. Now, where's the soap?"

Iris might have protested but found the soap and a pan for the sink. "Here, my lady. I'll find towels for drying."

"Good." Surveying the daunting task before them, she tied an apron around her waist and said, "Well, let's get to it."

After what seemed like hours later, Anne set the last dish onto the drainboard to dry. She picked up the dishpan and carried it to the backdoor to dump the dirty water. She set the pan on a small table, opened the solid wood door, picked up the pan, pushed open the screen door with her backside, and swung the pan to her left. Too late, she saw Morgan walking up to the back of the house. She narrowly missed drenching him.

"What do you think you're doing?" he shouted.

"Cleaning up," she said, raising her voice to the level he had used. She saw the spot on the side of his head and was reminded of their earlier encounter where he had startled her. "Must you always skulk around the rear entrance? Don't you ever use the front door?"

CHAPTER 6

$\mathcal{M}$organ took in Anne's level of dishevelment and wondered what the devil she'd been up to. Damp curls clung to her face, her cheeks were bright red, while the front of her dress looked like she'd tried to wash it while wearing it. He followed her inside and saw immedi ately what she'd been doing. There were a few plates left to be dried, but the rest were stacked on the table to be put away.

"You've been busy."

"It was the least we could do, since Mollie was up all night." She picked up a plate and wiped it with a damp towel. When she'd stacked it with the others and picked up another, she said, "She was practically asleep on her feet, so we sent her to bed."

"That was thoughtful, I know she appreciates it." From their recent history, he held his tongue before saying something she could take the wrong way. It was obvious she was unfamiliar with the task of dishwashing, and he admired her for stepping up to help Mollie. Had he misjudged her?

Iris came into the kitchen. "My lady, I've put a clean cloth on the table and next I'll put the dishes back into the buffet." She jumped when she saw him, and said, "Oh, Mr. Grant, it's nice to see you. Can I get you anything?"

"No, thank you. I was hoping to take Anne on a brief tour of the town."

"I think that's a fine idea." Mollie came into the room. She drew a large pot of water, set it on the stove, and lit a fire. "I'm going to boil water for the rest of the day and prepare dinner for those who'll be here. Leftovers will be for supper tonight."

"Mollie, I am more than willing to assist you," Anne said. "What can I do?"

"Not a thing I can think of. As soon as the water boils, I'm going over to the doc's office to check on Walt. Dinner may be a little late today, but that shouldn't be a problem."

Clasping her hands together, Anne said, "Well, then, Morgan, I would like to see the place that will be my new home."

"Good," he answered. "Take the time you need, there's no rush."

ANNE TOOK in her reflection in the free-standing mirror and was pleasantly pleased with the way she had turned out. Iris had many talents as a lady's maid and never ceased to amaze her at what she could accomplish.

Thanks to Iris, in a short amount of time, she was more than presentable in her travel suit that miraculously didn't look like it had been worn for three days, and her hair had been styled slightly off her face into a chignon. Her hat deftly placed, she pulled on her gloves and made her way back downstairs.

Morgan stood at the countertop peeling potatoes and dropping each one into a pot of water. Odd to see a man in the kitchen. At Higby, they only had women as cooks and kitchen staff.

She cleared her throat when he didn't he didn't acknowledge her presence, and said, "I'm ready if you are."

He turned as she spoke. Drawing an almost imperceptible breath, his thorough perusal of her, as he dried his hands on a towel, almost made her bolt from the room but she stood fast. Good or bad, she was Lady Medvale and even in this country that should mean something. She would see that it did.

"Yes, I believe you are." He nodded and said, "I'll put on my coat."

They walked the short distance to the edge of town where the hum and buzz of activity continued much the same as it had been yesterday when they arrived. She had never seen this many people in one place before, even in London. It was both exciting and frightening.

Holding tightly to his coattail, she walked close behind him so as to not get separated from him. After they passed one of the many oil company offices and the many men trying to get inside, she asked, "Is it always like this?"

"Ever since they struck oil at Spindletop, yes. Come on." He took her by the hand and ducked into the next store. "It'll be warmer in here and you can look around at the fancy gewgaws."

She quickly glanced at her surroundings and realized she was in the mercantile. The aisles were bordered with bolts of fabric, notions, ribbons, and lace. She marveled at the size and content of the business.

"This is amazing," she said, as she ran her gloved fingers over a bolt of satin. "The choices are staggering, and what is that wonderful smell?"

"I imagine something just came from the oven. Hortense has a small bakery in the back of the store." He slipped his hand beneath her elbow and asked, "Shall we go find out?"

"Oh, yes, please."

Her mouth was watering by the time they reached the small area containing two small tables in front of a counter. A tray holding freshly baked scones sat to the side. In the midst of the chaos and barbarism outside, she had fallen into a piece of heaven.

A short, round woman with red hair appeared behind the counter and said, "Hello, love, could I interest you in a nice, hot scone?"

Anne thought the resemblance to Mrs. Flaven, their cook at Higby Castle, uncanny. Add in the woman's perfect English accent, and for just a moment, she was home.

Morgan spoke before she had a chance to answer. "Hortense Blinebry, this is my fiancée, Lady Anne Medvale of England."

"Pleased to meet you, my lady. You haven't been here long, now, have you?"

"My maid and I arrived yesterday." The words sounded strange as she voiced them. So much had happened already. Had it only been twenty-four hours?

"Well, you've had a shock, I imagine. I've lived here twenty years and my senses are reeling, I'll tell you." The woman smiled, as she picked up a scone. "Have a seat and I'll bring you a plate and a nice cup of hot tea."

"Thank you, Mrs. Blinebry."

Morgan carried the cups and the teapot to the table, while Hortense brought the scones. When she turned to leave them alone, he said, "Join us, Hortense. I'm sure Anne would enjoy getting to know you."

"And I her. My lady?"

Anne removed her gloves to spread some jam onto her scone and said, "Do sit and chat. I admit your voice is making me homesick for the Queen's language. Where are you from?"

"Cambria, my lady."

"Do you miss it? Home, I mean?"

"Some," Hortense said wistfully. "But, I imagine it's changed from when we were last there."

"Is Albert around?" Morgan interrupted.

"He's unloading a wagon out back."

"If you'll excuse me, ladies, I'll go find him."

"So, Albert is your husband?"

"He is, for thirty years, but he'll always be a prince to me."

Anne smiled at the woman's reference to Prince Albert, Queen Victoria's husband. "I suppose we are all looking for our prince, so to speak."

"Well, my lady, if I'm not speaking out of turn, Morgan Grant is a prince among men." Hortense leaned forward, her elbows on the table. "You are a fortunate woman."

"Apparently," Anne said. "Mollie feels so, too."

"I don't know what circumstances brought you here, my lady," Hortense said, pushing away from the table, "But, Morgan is a good man and you could do much worse."

"Thank you, Mrs. Blinebry, it is a pleasure to meet you."

"Welcome, ma'am." Hortense stood, gathered the teapot and a cup, and said, "I must get back to my customers."

"Of course. I've enjoyed our conversation." Anne stood, slipped her gloves back on, and saw Morgan a few aisles over where he was talking with two men. She nodded when they connected and joined him.

"Gentlemen, Lady Anne Medvale. Anne this is Albert Blinebry, proprietor of Blinebry's Mercantile, and Ellis Barton, our preacher."

"Your wife is lovely, Mr. Blinebry," she said as she shook hands with both men. After Mr. Blinebry excused himself, she asked, "Mr. Barton, I was under the impression you were not in town."

"I was out checking on a few members of our congregation, but my wife's sister sent word she needed me at home." Accepting a bag from a clerk, he looked inside, and then turned his attention back to Morgan. "I'll take these home to Mary. I'll be available for the time we discussed."

"Thanks, Ellis."

"Do your plans include me and were you planning on including me?" She realized she was the reason for her predicament, but she absolutely refused to be dictated to or pushed, something Morgan Grant may as well realize sooner than later.

"Of course, and I was—I-I do," he stammered. "I was just talking to Brother Barton, and he can marry us this afternoon."

She glanced to her right, focused on a tray of delicate, satin-pink pearl buttons, and then closed her eyes. This was going to happen, needed to happen, whether she was ready or not.

"Anne, have you changed your mind?"

Slowly, she opened her eyes and rested her hand on his forearm. "No, I haven't changed my mind. Since refusing your offer isn't an option before me, and I did say today . . ." Her voice trailed off along with any hope of retaining her former life.

He lifted her chin with two fingers, and softly asked, "So, Lady Medvale, will you be my wife?"

Meeting his gaze, she answered resolutely, "Yes, Morgan, I will marry you."

"Good, shall we say two o'clock? Will that give you enough time to get ready?"

"Yes, I believe so. Can you make sure our trunks have been delivered?"

"We can do that on the way back to Mollie's."

"Two o'clock this afternoon!" Mollie exclaimed. "So that's the reason I felt the need to bake a cake."

Anne immediately felt guilty for telling Mollie of their plans after Morgan had left her at the boarding house. She had enough to do without adding one more thing to her list.

"Please, don't go out of your way," she said. "Nothing special is required." *Because this marriage is nothing special.* It was merely a means to an end. Nothing more, nothing less.

Mollie's attitude was effervescent and infectious, as she answered,

"Nonsense. We've had far too little to celebrate lately. Now, you and Morgan will come here after the ceremony and we'll have cake and coffee to mark the occasion."

"That will be lovely," Anne conceded.

Someone knocked on the front door. Mollie opened it and splayed her hand to her bosom. "Mercy, two trunks? Well, bring them on in and take them up to the room at the top of the stairs."

After the men had deposited the trunks, Anne walked to the bottom step and said, "Iris, I'll need you to help me dress for the ceremony."

"Of course, my lady, I'm right behind you."

Anne opened the first trunk and found the wedding dress she intended to wear right away. It was of white silk, organdy, and metallic thread. Handmade lace graced the bodice and formed the sleeves. Her father had complained about the cost of the Paris original but, being so anxious to marry her off, had paid the bill none the less.

She carefully laid the dress across the bed, smoothing out the wrinkles, then set out the jewelry from the top tray. Next, she pulled the satin slippers from the shoe bags. They matched her dress perfectly but, with the hem of her travel suit completely ruined, she wouldn't wear them. She couldn't bear to think of ruining them in the oil-soaked, mud streets.

"What do you think?" she asked Iris when she came into the room.

"I would have laid it out for you, my lady."

"I know, I wanted to." Anne shook out the organdy covered lace sleeves and brushed at the wrinkles in the skirts. "Is it too much? Should I wear another gown?"

"No, this is the one you should wear." Iris picked up the gown and held it in front of Anne, and then turned her to face the mirror. "See, this is perfect, my lady, and if you don't wear a wedding dress on your wedding day, when would you?"

"You're right."

As if Iris had read her mind, she added, "Don't worry, my lady, we'll take care not to let the hems get soiled."

Anne sat at the small dressing table, removed her earrings, and held out her arm for Iris to unfasten her bracelet. Iris removed the pins from the chignon and began brushing her hair.

"I don't have a hat for the occasion, or a veil. Is there something you can do?"

"Well, I could pin your diamond bracelet into the front like we did at Christmas or . . ." Iris went to the top tray in the opened trunk, picked through the cache of necklaces, rings, and bracelets. She chose a couple of pieces and joined Anne. "What do you think if I gather your hair onto the top of your head and wind Lady Margaret's pearls into the curls?"

"I think that would be lovely, and grandma-ma will be there with me."

"Hey, doc?" Morgan entered the doctor's office through the same back door he'd used earlier this morning.

"We're in here."

Morgan recognized the voice and followed it to find the marshal sitting up in the bed smoking a cigarette. His left shoulder was bandaged, and his left arm wrapped next to his body.

"Well, this isn't what I expected to find." Morgan grinned and stepped closer to shake the man's hand.

Walt placed the cigarette between his lips, gripped Morgan's hand in return, and asked, "Disappointed?"

"Pleasantly surprised."

Doc Harper came into the room. "Don't let him fool you, he still has some recovering to do, but he'll mend."

"Good. I've been trying to give his job away but can't find anybody dumb enough to take it."

"Not even you?"

"Especially me," Morgan said. "I'm getting married today."

"Took my advice, did you?"

"Had nothing to do with you, Walt. Came to the decision myself."

"Whatever you need to tell yourself, but I planted that seed and I'm here to see it bloom." Walt swung his legs over the side of the bed and set his feet on the floor. Behind a grimace, he said, "Hand me my shirt."

"Walt, you need to stay put," Doc said.

"You're taking me over to Mollie's later anyhow. We might as well go on and go, 'cause I intend to be the one to give her away."

Morgan shared the doc's frustration at the man's stubbornness. While he understood Walt wanting to have control over his life, he also understood Doc's concerns. "Walt, our plans are to be married in the preacher's parlor. Doc doesn't want you to be jostled around that much."

"I get it," Walt said, "But I'm not going to let a couple of stitches—"

"Doc!"

Morgan followed Doc Harper to the main room that served as Doc's reception and found the preacher standing just inside.

Doc closed the door and asked, "What's wrong, Ellis?"

"I'm glad you're here, Doc. Mary's got a high fever, can you come over right away?"

"I'll grab my bag."

"Ellis, I'm sorry about Mary," Morgan said. He could tell by the look on the man's face he was worried about his wife. "Don't worry about the ceremony this afternoon. We'll get with you in a few days when she's feeling better."

"I appreciate that, I—"

"Nonsense!" Mollie said firmly as she bustled into the room. "Let's wait for Doc to say what's wrong with Mary, before you two go off and ruin the afternoon.

"Now, Ellis go with Doc to check on your wife. Morgan, you

help me get Walt over to the Mollie B."

He followed her to the back of the office. "Look, I'd rather not postpone our plans, but we may have to."

Mollie stopped, turned, and took hold of his arm. "Listen to me," she said, her tone low and stern. "That girl has been dressing since you left the house. You'll be married today, if you have to join the Methodist church to have the Pastor perform the ceremony."

"We'll see." Morgan matched Mollie glare for glare. Her defense and support of her ladyship was admirable, but she was pushing him too hard, and he'd become very good at planting his feet.

Although, she had given him another small insight into Lady Anne Medvale. Little by little, he was chipping away at her armor and he found, increasingly, he was looking forward to discovering the woman beneath the façade.

CHAPTER 7

Morgan walked into the living room to check the clock on the mantle just as Doc Harper came through the front door.

"Doc, how's Mary?"

"She's doing better after we got some of the covers off her. I think all the quilts were holding in the heat making her hotter," he said. "I gave her some aspirin and her temperature has already lowered."

"That's good news." Morgan took the medical bag, as Doc shrugged out of his coat.

"Yes, but I still don't know for sure what's ailing her and, as long as she has a fever, she's contagious."

Morgan started thinking of an alternative plan for the ceremony, one that didn't involve him joining another church, when the front door opened, and the preacher walked inside carrying his Bible.

Doc quickly asked, "Ellis? Is Mary all right?"

"She's some better, thanks to you and the Lord," Ellis said and grinned. "She told me to stop bothering her and get to work. Morgan, I've been thinking, though, the church building is cold, and the stove is broken. I don't know if I can get it fixed today."

Mollie came into the room, hands on her hips, and said, "Don't overthink it gentlemen, we'll have it at the Mollie B."

"You've done enough, Mollie. I don't want to put you out." "Nonsense, I've put together a small reception, and your bride's already there, it simply makes sense. Now, if y'all can get Walt over to the house before he does it under his own steam, I'd appreciate it."

A short time later, when they'd gotten Walt over to the boarding house, Morgan saw Mollie was right. The dry warmth from the fireplace chased February's damp chill. Ribbons adorned the mantle and a few chairs had been added to the parlor. A cake sat on the dining room table, as did Mollie's prized silver tea service.

"What do you think?" Mollie said, as she set out plates beside the forks and spoons.

"I think it's a lot of fuss, but then none of this is about me."

"I always said you were a smart man." She stood back a short distance, looked at the table, and said, "I'm going upstairs to check on your bride. Gather everyone into the parlor, would you? And don't forget your coat, I loaned you one of Bert's and hung it on the back of Walt's chair."

"Yes, ma'am."

He made the observation that he was glad Mollie was on his side for he wouldn't want to have her as an enemy. She ruled everything in her path. He thought about the thing that currently controlled him, his job as a deputy marshal while Walt's shoulder was on the mend.

So far, today, the other deputies had been able to keep the town quiet. He hoped the peace continued through the ceremony and reception, but the back of his neck itched and that never meant anything good.

ANNE LOOKED up through the lace scarf anchored in her hair with hairpins to see Mollie in the mirror's reflection when she opened the door and entered the room carrying a box. She turned around slowly, so Mollie could see the results of Iris's efforts.

"What do you think?"

Mollie set the box on the bed and then held out the silk, organdy, and lace trimmed skirt. "I think Morgan Grant is going to swallow his tongue. Anne, you are absolutely breathtaking."

Wouldn't that be a sight to behold?

Aloud, she said, "All the credit goes to Iris. She is deftly adept at turning a sow's ear into a silk purse."

"Well, dear, I hardly think that applies to you." Mollie removed the lid to the box and said, "I don't know how you're fixed for old, new, borrowed, or blue, but I do know the flower situation in this town. Would these work for old or borrowed?"

Anne took the bouquet of flowers from Mollie, gently touching the hand tatted petals nestled among green silk ribbons. "These are so beautiful, Mollie. Where did you get them?"

"It was dead of winter when Bert and I married putting us in the same predicament as you. My grandmother made my bouquet for me."

"These make a perfect borrow, I will be honored to carry them." She hugged her new friend, and then said, "The pearls Iris used in my hair and on my ears, are from my grandmother, so that would be old, and the lace gloves are new. That leaves blue and a sixpence for my shoe."

"I have it." Iris went to the trunk and pulled out a length of sky-blue satin ribbon. "Here, my lady. Shall I tie this around your waist?"

"Yes," Anne said. "This marriage has enough going against it, I'd rather not jinx it further." When that was done, she asked, "How far is it to the preacher's house? I have on my day shoes, due to the mud, and I'll need help holding up the hem, so my dress doesn't get ruined."

"Oh!" Mollie raised her hand to her cheek. "In all the hub- bub going on downstairs, I forgot to tell you. You'll be married here in the parlor, and if you don't mind, Walt would like to give you away."

Anne's eyes welled with tears at the sweet gesture. Her throat tightened, but she managed to say, "How lovely."

While she sat on the stool to change her shoes, Mollie dug into her pocket and handed Anne a coin. "Here, I don't have a silver sixpence for good fortune and prosperity, but I do have a copper penny."

"That will do nicely." Anne took the coin, slipped it into her satin slipper, and stood. Looking from one woman to the next, she said, "I guess I'm ready."

MORGAN TURNED toward the stairs when the guests let out a collective gasp. Lady Anne Medvale was a vision in white froth. He knew she'd been coming here to get married so he shouldn't be surprised, but the wedding dress caught him off guard.

She continued toward him, stopping beside Walt's chair. The injured marshal stood, walked the couple of steps to where Morgan waited, and placed her hand in his. With a nod to Ellis, he reclaimed his seat.

Her hand visibly shook giving him the impression that, if he let go, she would fly into a million pieces. So, he held fast, squeezing her fingers to ground her.

Ellis whispered, "Are we ready?"

Morgan snagged her glance. "Anne?"

She looked at him and then Ellis, and said, "Yes."

Ellis placed his hand atop theirs and began the ceremony. "Folks, you're gathered here to witness the marriage between Morgan Grant and Anne Medvale. If there are no objections, we'll begin." He looked around the small room and hearing none, he said, "Repeat after me:

"Will you, Anne, have Morgan, to be your husband? Will you love him, comfort and keep him, and forsaking all others, remain true to him as long as you both shall live?"

"I will."

Morgan reached into the pocket of his jacket and pulled out a ring. He placed it on the ring finger of her left hand and repeated the words Ellis said.

"With this ring, I thee wed, and with all my worldly goods I thee endow. In sickness and in health, in poverty or in wealth, till death do us part."

"I now pronounce you man and wife. Morgan, you may kiss your bride."

Morgan slowly lifted the lace veil and wondered if he should kiss her. He ran the risk of upsetting her no matter which choice he made.

She leaned in and said quietly, "It's quite all right. I understand if you would rather not kiss me."

He rested his hands on her shoulders, angled his mouth over hers, and whispered, "It's my honor."

ANNE IMMEDIATELY FELT his absence when he broke their kiss. She braced herself on his arm, not realizing she had leaned into him.

"Are you all right?"

She glanced up at him when he spoke to her. Hearing the concern in his voice, she said, "I am, I'm just . . ."

"Rattled?"

She saw the mischief in his eyes and the up tilt of his mouth at the corner and knew he was teasing her, trying to get a response from her. Well, she'd had a response all right. For the second time in two days, heat coursed throughout her body. But Morgan Grant had confidence oozing from his ears and she refused to feed his ego. She smiled and answered him before she melted into a puddle at his feet.

"No, I'm hungry. I've been thinking about Mollie's cake and finger sandwiches since before I came downstairs."

He seemed to only miss a half-beat before saying, "Then, we

should get you to the table without delay. I've already had to carry you once this week."

The scoundrel. Was he now insinuating she was too heavy? Why the last time she knew, she was barely 8 stone 8. She came close to letting him have it and then she noticed his barely-there grin, just as their guests gathered around them. In the future, she would need to learn to read his face for his mood. That would save both of them from an embarrassing tongue lashing.

Mollie interrupted the ladies and their questions about Anne's dress when she said, "Why don't we go to the dining room for the reception? I'd like Anne to see we have some manners in this oil swamp we call a town."

"Now, Mollie," Anne said, "I'd like to think most people aren't defined by where they are from, even me."

"That's the truth, for certain." As she ushered the women into the dining room, she glanced behind her and said, "Morgan? Bring the men in, too."

Anne gasped as she saw the table Mollie had decorated. Her beautiful silver service anchored the table setting, with the cake sitting front and center. The teapot, hand painted with lavender flowers, was nestled to one side among matching cups and saucers. Similarly-patterned dessert plates, along with silver forks and spoons flanked to the left.

Iris entered the room from the kitchen carrying a tray with small sandwiches. She set them on a serving table, smiled, and said, "Congratulations, my lady."

"Thank you." Anne hugged her. The friendly gesture was almost never done by a Medvale, especially with a maid or other servant, but she and Iris had become so much more to each other. "I don't know when you had time to help with all of this. Apparently, your talents truly are limitless."

Iris smiled. "It was nothing at all, my lady."

Mollie clapped her hands. "Anne, dear, if you and Morgan would cut the cake?"

Anne picked up the knife, and when Morgan made no move toward her, she whispered, "You are supposed to help me do this."

"Why?"

"It is a tradition. Cutting the cake together symbolizes our commitment to each other."

He placed his hand over hers on the knife handle, slipped his left arm around her waist, and whispered into her ear, "Like this?"

She didn't know why he affected her the way he did. Perhaps it was his warm breath in her ear that sent cool shivers down her neck and spine or the intimate way he looked into her eyes, like they were the only two people in the room. Whatever the reason, it took all the control she had to keep her hand from trembling beneath his. Would she always react this way to his touch?

"It's all right, Anne," he whispered. "I'm committed to you and I'll always protect you."

After the last guest had been served, Walt lifted his cup and said, "A toast to the newlyweds. Congratulations, Anne, and Morgan, on this special day. As you embark on this new journey together, always keep in mind that your first duty to each other is to listen. Love will find its way."

"Thanks, Walt. We—" "Boom!"

Before Morgan finished his response, the loudest explosion Anne had ever heard rocked the house. Everyone standing, either dropped or were knocked to the floor by the blast. A second blast followed, its report louder than the first.

Morgan was the first to regain his feet, with the others responding soon after. He pulled her into his arms and said, "Stay here with Mollie and Walt. I'll be back as soon as I can."

With a quick kiss to her forehead, he was gone. She stood in the middle of shattered chandelier glass and the shards from the broken dishes. She said a quick prayer for everyone outside that may have been injured and wondered if Morgan would come back to her. Would she be a widow on the same day she became a bride?

CHAPTER 8

Morgan saw nothing but flames and billowing black and grey smoke when he ran out to the front yard of the boarding house. As he sprinted toward the depot, he realized an oil rig had exploded and the fire was threatening everything in its path, including two other wells and the Mollie B. He didn't have to go far before he encountered the town's volunteer firefighters and others running toward the fire.

Another of Walt's deputies, Bob Allen, stopped him and, shouting over the roar of the fire, said, "I'm headed to get folks out of the buildings on this end of town." He pointed over his shoulder. "Bill's gathering folks into the church sanctuary, and Ted's working on keeping the peace. What else do you want us to do?"

"Keep going," he said cupping his hands around his mouth, so he'd be heard. "I'm going back to Mollie's and clear the house!"

He choked and gasped his way to the Mollie B. Each step he took brought the flames nearer so that it looked like the back of the house was fully engulfed. When he burst through the front door, the living and dining room looked exactly as he'd left them, except no one appeared to be in the house.

"Anne? Mollie? Walt?" He called all their names but got no response. He breathed easier and headed to the back of the house through the kitchen where he saw all the windows had been blown out. When he hit the back steps, he realized the house wasn't on fire. Not yet, at least. However, the sight that greeted him was heart wrenching.

Walt, using his good arm, was digging a trench a short distance from the fence line from the property, Mollie stood in the middle of several buckets, some with water, some empty. Neither Anne or Iris were in sight.

Running up to Mollie, he shouted, "Where are Anne and Iris?"

"Down by the creek getting water. We've got to keep the house from burning!"

He knew the probable devastating outcome, and so did she. But she was so intent on saving her house, she couldn't see the futility of their actions.

"Mollie!" he said grabbing her by the shoulders. "Stop! Grab Walt and wait for me out in front on the street."

"But I have to . . .?" Her voice trailed off as she looked from the house to the fire.

"You can't save her." When she looked up at him, he said, "Now do what I told you and wait for me out front. I'll get the girls."

Before she could answer, Iris reached them dragging two half-full buckets beside her. "Oh, Marshal Grant! Saints preserve us, you're here."

"Where's Anne?"

Picking up two empty buckets, she said, "She's in the creek scooping out the water. I have to get these to her."

He took the buckets from her and tossed them to the side. "Go with Mollie, now. I'll get Anne."

The path was muddy and slick from the water Iris had spilled, and he came close to joining Anne in the middle of the creek. Still wearing her wedding dress, she stood in ankle deep water, mud on her face and her backside. At that moment, amidst the chaos surrounding them, he'd never seen a more bedraggled lady or a more appealing woman. He offered her his hand.

"Morgan, thank God." She reached for his hand and promptly fell forward landing face-down in the water. Scrambling to her feet, she uttered, "Crikey!"

"Come on, Anne, we have to get out of here. It isn't safe." He dipped down and lifted her into his arms. Immediately, she began to kick and wriggle until she slid out of his arms and onto the ground. She landed with a thud largely due to the amount of water absorbed by the material in her dress. "What are you doing?"

Scrambling to stand, her back ramrod straight, she said, "I can walk on my own two feet. I wouldn't want you to strain your back." Gathering fistfuls of her skirt, she stormed off toward the street.

They reached the others just as another, smaller explosion sounded. This time it came from the direction of the train depot. He had to find out what was burning and how he could help.

"I heard the church is putting folks up for a while, at least until we can get this under control." Not one but three of them started to protest. He'd anticipated resistance from Mollie and Walt but, apparently, his bride truly did have a stubborn streak. He raised his hand, and said, "I expect all of you to get to the safety of the church, so I can do my job. Walt, someone needs to take a look at your shoulder. Looks like you've busted those stitches."

Without further conversation, he turned and walked toward what surely must be Hell.

ANNE once again lifted her wet clothes to make the trek across town. She had almost put up a fuss and insisted on staying with Morgan, although she knew he was right. It was dangerous, and he couldn't do his job with her underfoot. His job. But being a marshal, she reminded herself, wasn't really his job.

Along the way, Mollie diverted them to Doc Harper's office. Once inside, she said, "Walt, go into the surgery so I can have a look at that shoulder. Anne, there are blankets in the cabinet in the next room, and Iris, I'll dance at your wedding if you'll make us some coffee."

Anne retrieved the blankets and joined Mollie in the surgery. Spreading one across Walt's legs, she focused on a painting of a farmhouse hanging on the wall across the room, anything to avoid the scene before her. She had never been good at anything medical, thank heavens she had never had to be.

After another couple of minutes, Mollie said, "There you go, Walt, I'm just about done here. Anne, would you tie this sling behind his neck?"

When she'd done as Mollie had asked and Walt was sitting up, she said, "I'm sorry about your house."

"Me, too. I just hope and pray they can get the fires put out sooner than later, before there's more injury and destruction."

Anne watched as the older woman place the soiled bandages and sponges to be cleaned or thrown away into a porcelain basin. Her movements were slow, methodical, and mesmerizing, and suddenly, Anne felt all the energy drain out of her. It seemed impossible that so much could have happened in only two days. Two days and three months since her life had fallen apart.

Realizing she wasn't the only one who'd had her life ripped to shreds, she pulled herself together and said, "It's so calm and quiet in here, like there is nothing untoward beyond these walls. I wonder how it's going out there, I wonder . . ."

"I don't know, but know this," Mollie said, "Morgan is strong and careful. He will be all right."

"I want to believe you," Anne said, "But we won't know for certain until we can see him, and he doesn't know yet we're here instead of the church."

"Don't worry love, he'll find us." Mollie sniffed the air and visibly perked up. "Smells like Iris has the coffee ready. Shall we have a cup and then get ready for any casualties Doc brings?"

"Yes."

Anne sat at the table in the small kitchen and closed her eyes. What she wouldn't give for a bed and a pillow. Her own bed in her old room at Higby Castle would be lovely, but those days were gone forever. She thought then about her trunks filled with some of her favorite trinkets, jewelry, and all her clothes. Would they survive, or would they perish along with Mollie's house?

"Here you go, my lady." Iris set a cup of hot coffee in front of her. "I fixed it like you like with sugar and plenty of milk."

She looked up and smiled. "You're a life saver, truly."

The hot brown beverage smelled strong enough to walk by its self, Anne wasn't sure she wanted to drink it, tea would have been her drink of choice, but when Mollie raved about the robust flavor, she took a sip. The taste surprised her and warmed her all the way down. She had just begun to perk up when the front door burst open.

"Anne? Mollie!" Morgan shouted as he ran inside.

Anne stood as she answered, "We're in the kitchen!" She greeted him, startled by his oil and soot smudged appearance but pleased to see him none the less. And wasn't that a surprise? She pulled out her chair for him and said, "You found us."

"Yes, but I was worried when you weren't at the church."

"Mollie thought it best to come here to take care of Walt's shoulder, and be ready to help Doc with the wounded if necessary."

"That makes sense. I was just worried when I couldn't find any of you."

Mollie put a cup of coffee into his hand. "How is it out there? Is the fire under control yet?"

"No, but the wind is helping to keep the flames from the town and your house for the time being. They were able to disconnect a burning car and push it out away from the train station." He drained the cup of its contents, took a deep breath, and continued, "The well, however, is still burning out of control. Word's been sent to get help in capping it off."

She wished she knew what to do for him. Another thing she wasn't good at, meeting other people's needs. She placed her hand on his arm and said, "You look very tired. Is there anything I can do for you? Would you like to lie down?"

"I feel like I've been yanked through a knot hole backwards." His initial answer to her was clipped and short but, as if he had second thoughts, he covered her hand and said, "Thank you. I would like to sleep, but if I find a pillow with my name on it, I may not wake up until next week. Since the firemen have the fire contained, I need to make sure the rest of the town is under control." He stood, pushed in his chair, and walked to the door to leave.

Anne followed him. "Morgan?"

"Yes?"

"I just wanted to say be careful."

He gave her a smile and a wink. "Always."

A pounding on the door sounded before she could manage a response to his over confident statement. Morgan opened the door to Jacob Beasley's son whose words came out rapid fire.

"Marshal Grant, my pa sent me to tell you the Texas Rangers are here and there's a whole company of 'em and they want you to come right away!"

Anne wondered, as her new husband disappeared down the street in the red-gold glow of the still burning fire, would this truly be the end of this nightmare wedding day?

CHAPTER 9

Anne savored the luxury of having a bath in her room because she knew she would need to relinquish it soon. Iris and Mollie were waiting in line. Her ruined wedding dress lay in a heap on the floor along with the now blackened satin slippers. She would cry about it, if tears would do any good, but there was so much more to cry over.

Mollie's house hadn't burned, due to the winds keeping the flames at bay, but would be uninhabitable until the windows could be replaced. Morgan and a few of the men had retrieved their trunks and bags and brought them out to his ranch. They had arrived earlier this morning, from their temporary stay at Doc's house, and it had taken the better part of the day to get them all settled in. As was no surprise, Walt was proving to be the most challenging of the group, trying at every opportunity to get to the marshal's office.

A knock sounded at the door and, since she was expecting Iris, she said, "Come in. I'm afraid I've gotten in without my towel. Would you be a dear and hand it to me?"

Morgan's distinctive, deep baritone answered her from behind the tub. "Don't be startled, m'lady, it's me." He reached around for the towel and handed it to her.

"Thank you. Where is Iris?"

"She's watching Mollie change Walt's dressing. I didn't realize you were still in the bath, I just wanted to see if you needed anything."

Calmly, she draped the towel across the tub, inches above the waterline, hopefully to cover strategic areas. They hadn't yet consummated their marriage, and she was uncomfortable exposing herself to him.

"Good for her, I'm afraid I wouldn't make a good nurse."

"You could learn it," he said. "We can all do what we need to do."

"I suppose that is true."

He walked over to the fireplace, which stood directly in front of the tub, and began to stir the logs into a roaring fire. He added more wood, walked over to her, and caressed her cheek. "Enjoy your bath, I'll see you later."

"She didn't know exactly what he had meant by that, but as the door to the room closed, shivers shook her, and they had nothing to do with the temperature of the now frigid bathwater.

Morgan stepped into the hall and closed the door behind him. Seeing her in the tub had caught him completely off guard. He couldn't remember ever being so intrigued or wanting a woman so badly. The urge to steal a glance of her as she relined against the back of the tub had been too great and he'd succumbed against his better judgement.

Water droplets had glistened across her bare shoulders, wisps of damp curls lay against her face, and knowing what she'd tried to discreetly conceal with the towel had caused him such physical discomfort, it had made it difficult for him to leave the room. The most he'd been able to do was touch her cheek After a few minutes, he pushed away from the door and headed downstairs. He and Walt were expecting one of the Rangers to visit with their thoughts on why the oil well had exploded causing the fire.

Walt greeted him at the foot of the stairs. "I think we ought to go back to the office to see how things are going."

"I promised Doc I'd keep you here for a couple of days to give your shoulder time to heal. And quite frankly," Morgan said, "I'm not up to facing Mollie if I don't follow through on that promise. You know as well as I do the Rangers have the town under control."

"Yeah." Walt huffed out a sigh. "I don't want to face her either."

Morgan chuckled to himself to think one woman had the capability to rule with an iron fist. Yet the irony of that was, he'd married one such woman.

A short while later, Morgan saw a man ride up to the front gate on his horse. He motioned toward the window and said, "Here's our guy now."

"Good, we need answers."

Morgan opened the door to greet the lawman. "Ranger Pike, welcome."

"Deputy Grant, Marshal Fountain, it's good to see you."

Walt shook the man's hand and asked, "How's the investigation going?"

"Talking to the men working on the drill site, I believe we've come up with a timeline of events and reached a conclusion." He removed his hat and sat on the settee next to Walt. "Apparently, a roughneck, there's some debate which company he worked for, held a lantern over the top of a barrel to see what was in it and the flame from the lantern ignited the fumes."

"Did he make it?" Walt asked.

"No, he didn't."

Walt shook his head. "There's no accounting for fools and idiots."

"Yeah," Morgan said, "It never ceases to amaze me the number of 'em out there. Do you have an identification yet, Jim?"

"Just a first name. Seems your salon keeper, Beasley, knows

him as a troublemaker named, Percy. Do either of you recognize the name?"

"I don't think—"

"I do." Morgan said, interrupting Walt. "He came in on the same train as Anne. As a matter of fact, he was fairly obnoxious with both her and Iris. I had to show my badge and gun to get him to back down."

"We'll keep digging, trying to locate a positive identification and something about his background. Walt, in the meantime, a witness has come forward naming this same man as your shooter."

"Good," Walt answered. "I didn't know who he was, but I'd recognize him if I saw him again."

"So, would I, if he's the same man from the depot." Anne appeared in the doorway fresh from her bath, her dark hair in a long braid over her shoulder. "I couldn't help but over hear your conversation."

"Well ma'am, as it turns out, I doubt we'll need you to identify him. Marshal Fountain or one of the witnesses from the shooting can probably identify the body."

"I am sorry to hear he didn't survive, but he was a horrid man."

Morgan said, "Jim, this my wife, Anne, um Lady Anne Medvale Grant. Anne, Jim Pike, Texas Ranger."

"Pleased to meet you, ma'am."

"How long will you be here?" she asked.

"We'll be here for as long as we're needed. Speaking of which, I'd better get back to town." He bowed slightly and turned for the front door. Stopping before he reached the door, he pulled something from his jacket pocket and turned to Morgan. "Before I forget, this wire came for you."

Morgan took the envelope from him, shook hands, and held the door. "Thank you for the information. We do appreciate you making the trip out to keep us informed."

After the Ranger rode away, Morgan turned back into the room and opened the envelope. To his surprise, the telegram was from Malcom Carp, the Englishman. The message said he would reach Beaumont within a week. This was good news, as the arrival of Mr. Carp would give him time to get things squared away at the ranch and get Anne settled into her new home. It would be good if she could feel comfortable entertaining Mr. Carp.

"Not bad news, I hope?" Anne asked, as she took the Ranger's place on the settee beside Walt.

"No, it's good. The man I'm doing business with will arrive next week."

Walt stood, grabbed his cup, and headed out of the room. "I'm going to let you two keep on visiting, while I go do something important, like harass Mollie."

Morgan shook his head and said, "I'm sure that'll make her day."

Anne raised her eyebrows. "I was thinking the exact opposite."

He started to point out he was being sarcastic but decided against it. In time, they would learn each other and figure out how to get along. He hoped.

"May I ask what kind of business you are in?"

"I'm in the business of raising cattle and getting them to market."

"Oh, do you don your chaps and spurs and drive them up the Chisolm Trail?"

If she'd been anyone else, he might've thought she was teasing but she'd mentioned reading about Texas, and he knew she was serious.

"I rode the trail in the early days working with my pa," he said. "These days, with the railroad here, it's easier to load the cattle into a boxcar and get them to market."

"I see, and do you have many business partners?"

He wasn't accustomed to talking about his ranch or its commercial inner workings, much less sharing that information, but she was his wife and she had a right to know.

"Just the one at this time. I'm hoping, with our collaboration, to improve my herd."

"And that will happen how?" She gave him a demure smile and said, "I'm not completely naïve, I do know some things about animal husbandry and reproduction. I have visited farms near Higby Castle and Pa-Pa has a marvelous library."

"I see." Another puzzle piece to his bride and her history that made sense. He'd never considered the possibility she'd lived in a castle or that she had a well-rounded education. He didn't know what he'd expected if he was honest with himself. "I'm looking forward to introducing you to Mr. Carp. I'm hoping you can help him feel more at home while he's here."

"Who did you say?"

"Malcom Carp." Was it his imagination or did her breath hitch at his mention of the name? It was almost imperceptible, but he'd noticed a reaction. "Do you know him?"

"I believe we've been introduced."

He'd lost eye contact with her when she'd answered, which told him she hadn't been completely forthcoming. Why he didn't know, but he remembered when they'd first met, he'd gotten the feeling she hadn't told him everything.

"I thought probably you'd heard of him. I believe he's from York. Isn't that where you're from?"

"Yes, it is." She stood, glanced toward the hall outside the living room, and said, "I promised to help Mollie this afternoon. Please excuse me."

Morgan watched as Anne left the room. She was definitely keeping something from him, and he wanted to know what her secret was, especially by the time Mr. Carp arrived.

ANNE STEPPED to the door of the kitchen where Iris sat at the table with Mollie. "Iris, could you help me for a minute?"

"Of course, my lady." Iris followed her down the hall to her bed room. When Anne ushered her inside and closed the door, she asked, "How can I help?"

"You'll never guess who Mr. Grant's business partner is."

"Who is it?"

"Mr. Malcolm Carp."

Iris turned her head away and hid a grin.

"What's so funny?" Anne asked.

"A few of the maids downstairs, referred to him as fish lips."

"So did my sisters and I on the one occasion he came to Higby, with Mr. Smith, at Christmas." She tried to keep a straight face but laughed despite herself. "Well, be that as it may, he's privy to the reason for my leaving Higby for America. He could ruin me here, too."

"Yes, I suppose he could, my lady," Iris said, "My advice is to tell Mr. Grant everything before it's too late."

"You are right, Iris. I will do my best to find the right time to tell Mr. Grant the truth."

CHAPTER 10

$\mathcal{A}$nne awoke early on the day Malcolm Carp was to arrive, and she still hadn't found the right time to tell Morgan about knowing Carp or about her time in London. She had planned to tell him sooner than later, but the past week had gone by quickly with all they had needed to do to get the house ready.

If she didn't tell him this morning, he would think her a coward, and he would be right. Unfortunately, though, by the time she had dressed and gotten to the dining room for breakfast, Morgan and Walt had left for town. Panic was her only excuse, that, and self-preservation. Now, all she could do was wait for their return to know her fate.

To take her mind off her impending doom, she double checked the house, beginning with the room for Malcolm. When she reached the kitchen, Iris, Mollie, and Morgan's cook, Providencia were working on the lunch to be served to the men when they returned to the ranch with their English guest. The women worked well together laughing and talking about their tasks.

"May I help?"

Providencia answered, "Is going good, señora. We will serve a good lunch for you."

"I know you will." She smiled at the woman who had been with Morgan for a few years. "Since this all seems well in hand, I will go check the dining room."

The table looked as fine as they could make it. She was sure the butler from Higby would not approve, but she had to admit the simplicity of having fewer crystal stems, china, and silverware was freeing. The chairs were all appointed, and the table decoration of ivy would do. Now, she just had to await her fate.

MORGAN SETTLED Mr. Carp onto the wagon seat and climbed up beside him. Walt had gotten the all-clear from Doc Harper, so he had retrieved his horse at the livery and had gone back to work at the marshal's office. He hadn't known what the Englishman would bring with him in the number of trunks and bags, but he had nearly as much as Anne. The wagon bed was fairly full.

Finally settled in for the drive to the ranch, he asked, "How was your trip? Were the seas smooth?"

"Relatively speaking."

Just then, the left front wheel dipped into a hole causing the wagon to lurch. Morgan recovered control and said, "Probably smoother than this road we're on."

"Quite," Carp agreed. "However, this is common for a dirt road. I am curious though about the odors that plague the area. Is this normal?"

"Unfortunately, it is, with the vast number of wells surrounding the town." He slowed the horses to navigate a rough patch in the road, and then continued, "I think you'll find the air is much better at the ranch."

"Ah, more to look forward to. I have heard many stories, is this the wild west?"

Morgan grinned. "Not generally, but you wouldn't know it from the influx of wildcatters and roughnecks. On January tenth, with the discovery of oil at Spindletop, any resemblance to normal left our little town for some time to come.

"Walt, our city marshal, was shot in a street fight a couple of weeks ago."

"Then, this is the wild west in the truest definition." He looked around and asked, "How much longer until we reach your ranch"

"We've actually been on ranch property for a few miles, but the house is just ahead there."

Carp held onto the side and back of the wagon seat as the wagon traveled over some deep ruts in the road. "Well, it will be nice to get there and have a look."

Morgan pulled the wagon to the front gate, tied off the reins, and jumped to the ground. He walked around the rear of the wagon and met Carp at the gate. Together, they walked to the porch. When the front door opened, he smiled and said, "Mr. Carp, this is my wife—"

"Lady Anne Medvale." Carp gave a small bow and kissed her hand. "What are you doing in this God forsaken country?"

"Mr. Carp," Anne said. "Welcome to Grant Ranch. Won't you come in?"

Morgan stared from one to the other with his face hanging out. Why hadn't she told him how well she knew Malcolm Carp, especially when he'd specifically asked her that day when Ranger Pike had come to the house? She'd had ample time to voice that tidbit of information. Why hadn't she?

"This way, Malcolm, you can wash up for lunch," Anne said, leading their guest to the washroom.

Morgan waited for her to return, and then he said, "You didn't say how well you know our guest."

"Oh, surely I mentioned it."

"No, no you didn't., and I demand you tell me now."

Iris came to the living room. "Luncheon, my lady, Mr. Grant."

"Thank you, Iris."

Morgan followed Anne as she led the way into the dining room. Taking hold of her arm, he said, "Tell me how you know Carp."

"I don't intend to get into this right now." She glanced around him and said, "Malcolm, please come in and have a seat."

He watched her orchestrate the serving of their lunch knowing he'd made the right choice in marrying her for this specific guest and any other guests in the future. She was definitely accomplished in decorum and social settings, something he lacked.

He did, however need to feel he could trust her. He observed the exchange between the two of them through the meal, their banter about old times in England, and though they never mentioned anything specific about their past, he got the feeling there was much more to it than was being spoken about openly.

As soon as she returned from showing Carp to his room for the afternoon, he approached her. "Anne, come with me."

"Morgan, I don't have time, right now. I have to clean up and get ready to set the table for dinner."

He took hold of her arm and ushered her outside onto the porch. When she tried to pull free of his grasp, he only tightened his grip. "We'll talk here or in front of our guest where you can explain to me why you neglected to say how well you know him."

She tried once again to break free of his grasp and said, "I will not be bullied. Now, let go of my arm."

Morgan knew stubborn when he encountered it directly, so he let go and followed her as she took out across the front pasture.

Anne kept walking until she stopped against the fence surrounding another pasture. Their short walk hadn't given her near enough time to work up her courage. She felt his eyes on her and finally, she jumped off the edge.

"Morgan, I haven't told you everything about my past."

"I know," he said. "Or, at least, I assumed so. Why don't you tell me now?"

She searched his eyes but saw nothing except kindness. She had to tell him everything, even the sordid mess with Mr. Smith.

"Two years ago, when my two younger sisters became engaged, my father began bringing suitors to dinner and the occasional hunt. You see, it's the duty of a daughter to marry, and I think Pa-Pa believed I might never find a man who could handle me." She grinned at him and said, "I don't know if you've noticed, but I have a bit of a stubborn streak."

The corner of his mouth quirked up when he answered, "I'm starting to pick up on that."

"Well, I decided a year ago I wasn't going to let him dictate to me who I would spend the rest of my life with. One night, I ran away to London with Mr. Smith. He was prominent in government and was expected to be the next Prime Minister."

"It sounds like a good match, what happened?"

She started to walk along the fence line to help her concentrate better on the conversation. "Unfortunately, after being at the hotel alone, with Mr. Smith in a room nearby, I found out he was married. He only wanted to keep me as his mistress."

He stopped her with his hand on her arm. "Did he . . . touch you?"

"No, of course not! I was ruined just the same." She continued with her story. "Pa-Pa came to London to fetch me home and forbade me to leave Higby Castle. Then one day, Mr. Ballard showed up for dinner. His family had money and position in Boston society, so Pa-Pa brokered a deal for our marriage.

"The Ballard's wanted the marriage to take place in Boston and, since Pa-Pa was so determined, he agreed to their terms. Once we arrived, I found out Mr. Ballard wasn't the man I thought he was. I promptly called off the wedding and Pa-Pa closed my account at the bank when I refused to go back home. And that's how I became a mail order bride." Anne knew she had rambled, but her story was out now. A tremendous weight had been lifted from her shoulders. She wondered what he thought, but he just stood there staring off into the distance.

Finally, he spoke, "I have an idea, but first I need to know how Malcolm Carp figures into your story."

"He doesn't other than he is Mr. Smith's cousin and I was afraid he would give away my past."

Morgan reached for her hands and said, "Tomorrow we're going into town to send a telegram to your mother and father. You're going to tell them you're married and invite them to visit. Your father will come around."

"Do you think so?"

He pulled her into his arms and kissed her soundly. "I guarantee it."

Two months later, Anne rode next to Morgan in the new carriage he had bought to bring her parents to the ranch. They were due in today on the noon train. So much had happened since she had sent the telegram. First of all, he had been right about her father, and if she hadn't listened to him, they might have remained forever estranged.

Mollie had moved back into the Mollie B with Marshal Walt Fountain as her star boarder and close companion. The woman became girlish and practically giddy when talking about their close relationship.

The most recent occurrence was Iris and her new romance with a certain Texas Ranger, Jim Pike. It didn't appear she would be moving to live with her cousins in Dallas any time soon.

Morgan stopped the carriage at the depot, turned to her, and pulled her into his arms. "Are you happy, darlin'?"

"I am, truly." She loved being held close to him, her very own Texas rancher. She leaned back a bit and said, "I saw Doc Harper a few days ago. He told me something that's going to make you happy."

"You think so?"

"Yes, in about seven months you're going to be a father." She held her breath when he didn't answer right away. Boldly, for her anyway, she asked, "Aren't you happy?"

He smiled in that way she loved about him. "I am, truly, m'lady."

THANKS FOR READING MY BOOK.

If you enjoyed reading MAIL ORDER M'LADY, Brides of Beckham, please leave a review wherever you purchased the book. Reviews are important ways to say thanks to an author. They also let future readers know whether to buy the book.

FOR NEWS OF NEW RELEASES, contests, and events, please sign up for Carra Copelin's newsletter:

HTTPS://WWW.SUBSCRIBEPAGE.COM/S5M3U8

FIND CARRA COPELIN:
    http://carracopelin.com

HTTPS://WWW.FACEBOOK.COM/PAGES/CARRA-COPELIN-TEXAS-SKIES-AUTHOR/233861816666958

HTTPS://WWW.FACEBOOK.COM/GROUPS/CARRACOPELINSCORNER/

HTTPS://TWITTER.COM/#!/CARRACOPELIN

ACKNOWLEDGMENTS

This book is dedicated to the Mail Order Brides, Ranchers, Oil Field Workers, and Law Enforcement Agencies, all who helped make Texas the great state she is today.

I wish to extend an extra special thank you to my critique partner, beta reader, and my wonderful editor.

ABOUT CARRA COPELIN

I write contemporary and historical romances but, unlike so many other authors, I didn't write from childhood or read long into the night beneath the covers with a flashlight. I found romance novels as an adult. After reading about a million, I discovered numerous people residing in my head, all looking for a way onto the printed page.

I'm a member of Romance Writers of America, plus I'm a regular contributor to the blog, Smart Girls Read Romance.

My husband and I live in North Central Texas, in the Dallas- Fort Worth Metroplex where we enjoy our family and grandchildren. In addition to writing and researching, I enjoy my Bridge group, crochet, and tracking down our relatives through genealogy.

ALSO BY CARRA COPELIN:

Texas Code Series

CODE OF HONOR, Book One
THE LEGEND OF BAD MOON RISING

Brides of Texas Code Series Novellas

KATIE AND THE IRISH TEXAN, Book One
MATELYN AND THE TEXAS RANGER, Book Two
ANGEL AND THE TEXAN FROM COUNTY CORK, Book Three
FAITH AND THE TEXAS LAWYER, Book Four

Texas Holidays Series

LILAH BY MIDNIGHT
A Novella

A SANTA FOR CHRISTMAS
A Short Story
A BRIDE FOR CHRISTMAS
A Short Story
A FAMILY FOR CHRISTMAS
A Short Story

American Mail-Order Brides Series

Carra Copelim

LAUREL: Bride of Arkansas, #25
EMMELINE, Bride of Arkansas

Anthologies

A CHRISTMAS COWBOY TO KEEP